"It's dangerous for me to be here," she pointed out. "If anything happened to you or your girls because of me, I would—"

"You didn't bring this fight to my doorstep," he interrupted. "Someone else did and it's not your fault. Until we know who is behind this, I highly doubt we'll figure out why it happened. Unless, by some miracle, you get your memory back."

This didn't seem like a good time to say he was, in fact, the last person she wanted to bump into in Cider Creek despite the growing part of her that was happy to see him.

"That may very well be true," she said, thinking he had a good point. "I could make sure that I'm seen somewhere else. Draw these jerks away from you and your girls instead of toward."

"Careful, Hayes," he said. "I might actually think you've started caring about someone besides yourself."

# TROUBLE IN TEXAS

*USA TODAY* Bestselling Author

## BARB HAN

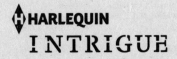
HARLEQUIN
INTRIGUE

All my love to Brandon, Jacob and Tori, who are the great loves
of my life. To Samantha for the bright shining light that you are.

To Babe, my hero, for being my best friend, greatest love and my
place to call home. I love you with everything that I am. Always
and forever.

To Shaq and Kobi, the best writing buddies ever.

**HARLEQUIN®**
**INTRIGUE™**

Recycling programs
for this product may
not exist in your area.

ISBN-13: 978-1-335-59121-0

Trouble in Texas

Copyright © 2023 by Barb Han

For questions and comments about the quality of this book,
please contact us at CustomerService@Harlequin.com.

Harlequin Enterprises ULC
22 Adelaide St. West, 41st Floor
Toronto, Ontario M5H 4E3, Canada
www.Harlequin.com

Printed in U.S.A.

*USA TODAY* bestselling author **Barb Han** lives in North Texas with her very own hero-worthy husband, three beautiful children, a spunky golden retriever/standard poodle mix and too many books in her to-read pile. In her downtime, she plays video games and spends much of her time on or around a basketball court. She loves interacting with readers and is grateful for their support. You can reach her at barbhan.com.

Visit the Author Profile page at Harlequin.com.

## CAST OF CHARACTERS

**_Reese Hayes_**—Can she remember what happened before a killer strikes again?

**_Darren Pierce_**—Will he walk away or risk his heart to help his former high school sweetheart?

**_Iris and Ivy Pierce_**—Will they be taken away from their father for his involvement in the case?

**_Aiden Archer_**—Why does he really stick to the family farm?

**_Alexander Archer_**—Does this family keep to themselves because they have something to hide?

**_Phillip Rhodes_**—Is this former camp counselor a serial killer?

## Chapter One

Even the slightest movement caused Reese Hayes's muscles to scream as she tried to rally herself awake and sit up. The sound of muffled voices penetrated the darkness. Did she know one of them? A sense of familiarity was followed by bone-penetrating terror. She had a headache so fierce she feared her brain might splinter.

Questions were hammering against the backs of her eyes. What happened? Where was she? Who was there?

The feeling of icy fingers wrapping around her brain made it next to impossible to think. A fog thicker than a San Francisco morning felt like a weighted blanket, pinning her to a hard, cold concrete floor. Groggy, Reese couldn't recall the events that had gotten her here...wherever *here* was.

Trying to move at all was as productive as spitting on a lawn and expecting the grass to stay green over a long summer with no sprinkler. The tight grip of claustrophobia seized the air in her lungs. Understanding the gravity of the situation, Reese mentally pushed aside her panic. She needed to focus—not on the fact that she was in a blacked-out room lying on a hard surface, unable to move without head-piercing pain, but she needed to mentally lock on to something she could control and hold onto for dear life.

Reese concentrated on her breathing. She listened to the voices, trying to make out whom they belonged to or, at the very least, get some information as to why she was there. Any hint of where she was would be welcomed, because she had no clue. She felt like an out-of-focus camera lens trying to zoom in on a target while multiple things were going on. The only thing she remembered was that she'd been outdoors and there'd been some kind of red building in the background, which made no sense under her current conditions. A staticky sound, like when Granny fell asleep without turning off the TV years ago, caused her muscles to tense.

*Breathe.* The idea was so much easier than the execution. She winced as she tried to feel around and gain her bearings. The voices became more distant until they almost faded completely. She listened for other sounds—a vehicle engine, the sound of water, anything. The wind whipped outside and when she really concentrated, she could hear rain droplets tapping against a windowpane. Good to know there could be an escape route nearby. She tried her best to ignore the nausea that was causing bile to burn the back of her throat. There was nothing she could do about that now.

For a split second, she prayed this wasn't happening, that this was a nightmare. But the pain confirmed that it was very much real.

Survival instincts kicked in. Adrenaline pumped through her veins. She attempted to roll onto her back.

Not much happened. The reason suddenly dawned on her. Her hands were tied behind her. Now that the shroud was lifting, she could feel her body better. Her eyes were adjusting to the darkness, too. And her senses were sharpening.

She tried to kick and immediately noted that her ankles were bound together. Was there something around that she could use to free her hands?

Squirming, she went headfirst into a wall. So much for ignoring her headache. Undeterred, she tried to feel around but there was nothing except for air behind her.

She heard the whisper of a male voice. He was close.

Reese strained to listen. She couldn't make out his words. There was nothing familiar about him. Was he the mastermind behind her kidnapping or just a willing accomplice?

What was the motive?

She had no real money to speak of other than a small amount that she'd saved up after working for the past ten years. She didn't own the kind of business that would warrant an abduction for extortion or revenge purposes. She didn't work in law enforcement. Her job in the Dallas fashion industry, which she'd started straight out of high school, wouldn't cause anyone to tie her up and leave her in an abandoned building.

Were there others here besides her? She was afraid to speak. Wouldn't she have heard something by now if there were others in here? There would have been breathing, or the sound of someone trying to move. Right?

The idea of being alone sent a cold chill racing up her back. She'd been a target. At twenty-eight years old, would she be too old for human trafficking? Since this couldn't be work-related and she had no idea what she'd been doing when the abduction had taken place, her thoughts snapped to things she'd read about. No one would take her for ransom. Hold on a minute, she might not personally have enough money to garner attention, but her family did. She was a Hayes and her grandfather, who'd been the patriarch of the family for as long as she could remember, had recently passed away.

Reese had been asked to come home to Cider Creek to discuss the ranch. Had she recently inherited boat-loads of money? That would certainly draw attention.

Wouldn't she be the first to know? Or was someone hedging a bet? While her mother was still alive, Reese highly doubted she was about to inherit the ranch. Sometime down the line, she would most likely be given a piece of the family legacy along with her siblings. She had no idea how well the place was doing. She'd left right after high school, just like her brothers and sister. Since their grandfather ran a tight ship and had built the business from scratch, she assumed all was well.

At this point, she guessed this could have to do

with a possible inheritance she had yet to learn about, or it came down to being a random occurrence. One might keep her alive. The other could make her dispensable if she created too much of a problem.

At least she was beginning to get some of her wits back. This was good. She could come up with a plan to get herself out of here and to safety. She had no idea where her purse might be, so that was an issue. She always carried two cell phones with her. One for A-list work clients and another for people like suppliers when she was helping put together an event. Those were B-level calls. Her A-list cell phone included VIPs in the industry, fashion magazine editors, top-level models who were hard to book, etcetera.

Most of the time, she had a cell glued to her palm. Where had hers gone? Because her A-list cell kept an almost constant buzz going. Even with an assistant, Reese had to handle the most important clients herself. She did well for herself but she was by no means a millionaire.

Why was it that she could remember what she did for a living, her family and the fact she had two cell phones, but couldn't for the life of her remember what she'd been doing to end up in a place like this? Trauma?

Reese might have been from the small town of Cider Creek originally, but she'd been living and working in downtown Dallas long enough to take necessary precautions. Safety measures that included locking doors and arming the alarm in her apartment every night. She knew better than to walk alone in an empty parking lot day or night, and had read enough warnings to remember that most abductions happened during the day. She was aware of her surroundings whenever she went out.

The sounds of some kind of commotion broke into her thoughts. A chair scraped across the concrete against the backdrop of mumbled curses and hurried footsteps.

A shot rang out before an engine roared and then tires spit gravel. Suddenly, one set of heavy footsteps filled the space. It was decision time. Reese could yell for help or stay quiet.

"Hello?" The familiar male voice and blast from the past sent momentary shock reverberating through her.

*Darren Pierce?*

"HELP ME. PLEASE."

Three words were all it took for time to warp and Darren Pierce to be transported back to the last day of high school. What the hell was Reese Hayes doing here? Even after all these years, he would recognize that voice. The desperation cut straight through his question—and his heart—as he made a beeline toward her.

The jerks who'd been squatting on his property had run off fast. But how had she gotten here?

Before his brain had time to come up with a response, he opened the door to a shed inside the old equipment building that he probably should have torn down years ago. The shutters had been closed and too little light came in from the building. The electricity had been knocked out in the last storm. He flipped on the flashlight app as Reese said his name. He flashed the light against the back wall and saw her. The second his gaze caught hers, all those old feelings surged, along with a threat to derail common sense. She'd walked out on *their* future, not just her family and the town. But, right now, she was in danger and he couldn't hold the past against her. Besides, if life had turned out differently, he never would have had the twins. Those girls were everything to him.

Darren closed the distance between them in two strides. He took a knee and ran the light the length of her body.

"Where does it hurt?" he asked.

"The back of my head feels like someone tried to drive a nail in it," she said in the voice that used to bathe him in warmth and light a dozen fires inside his chest. Now? He shoved aside those thoughts as he took stock of the situation. Her hands were behind her back. Her ankles were bound. The kind of anger that he might have acted on as a teenager if someone set him off pushed to the surface.

Darren immediately began ripping the electrical tape to free her hands. He moved to her feet next and freed them in a matter of seconds. Even in this light, she was still beautiful. Reese had a thick mane of dark-roast hair and espresso-colored eyes to match. Olive skin didn't hide the flush to her cheeks when she smiled or got nervous. He remembered the way her face flushed a second before their first kiss in the biology lab, when they'd been forced to stay after to help clean up. The teacher disappeared down the hallway and a moment had happened between them that had replayed in his thoughts far too often over the years.

As far as kisses had gone, theirs might have been innocent. Not much more than her cherry lips pressed against his own. But the effect had been a lasting imprint and the kiss he'd compared all others to. Then again, his first would always hold a special place in his heart. He'd written it off as to be expected, rather than go down the route of being irreplaceable.

The minute she could sit up, she wrapped her arms around his neck and held tight. "Thank you."

"No need for thanks," he reassured her. She didn't need to feel indebted to him. He did, however, have a growing list of questions. Her body was trembling—from fear, he expected, causing more anger to surface. Right now, he needed to get her out of there. "Can you walk?"

"I think so," she said as he lifted her to standing. Her knees almost immediately buckled. He steadied her, looping his arm around her. "Guess that's not as easy as I thought it was going to be."

"My horse isn't far," he said. He needed to get her out of this building, since he had no idea if those jerks were coming back or if they would bring friends. He'd spooked them away. His initial thought had been poachers. He ran into them from time to time on his small property. Growing up on a cattle ranch, he knew what to look for.

There'd been something different about this group, though.

"I might not be able to make it on my own," she said, flexing and releasing her fingers a few times, as if she was trying to bring back the blood.

"I already called the law to investigate, but I can't risk sticking around. We need to go. I can carry you," he said. "I'll give you my weapon in case they come back. You keep watch and buy us some time if anyone surprises us." Normally, he would be fine with sticking around for a fight, but the crown of her head was caked with blood. He wouldn't have moved her at all if there was a way around it.

She nodded.

He handed over his Colt .45, then scooped her up in his arms, ignoring the electrical currents that vibrated in his body. He chalked up the feeling to muscle memory as he bolted toward the door.

"Do you know what day it is?" he asked as he exited the old equipment building. He'd moved the shed inside to keep it out of the elements while he figured out what to do with both.

"Monday," she said with a whole lot of uncertainty in her voice. "Is that right?"

"Yes," he confirmed. At least she had the day of the week right. She knew his name, too, so that was another good sign she might not have a concussion. "What about the month?"

"December," she said, sounding a little more confident this time.

"Right again," he said. There was a good chance

she would be okay. He would still call in the doctor. "Do you know the people who ran off?"

"No," she said hesitantly.

"Any idea what that was about?" he asked as he approached the tree line, where he'd left Blaze, his mare.

"I have no clue," she said as she watched their backs while he sprinted through the woods toward his horse. Working on a horse ranch kept him fit. Plus, there were the extra workouts, which had to be temporarily suspended while he had the twins. He needed to be in shape to chase after those little angels.

"We'll figure it out," he said, glancing at her and seeing the physical pain that her trying to answer seemed to create. Her face twisted. Even in pain, she was more beautiful than he remembered.

But he also recalled how she'd stomped on his heart and never looked back, so he intended to keep his guard up.

## Chapter Two

Wrapped in arms like bands of steel, Reese surveyed the trees for fear one of the jerks who'd abducted her—and abduction was all she could think about at this point—would come back. No doubt, the bastards would be prepared for Darren this time.

Gratitude sprang to her eyes in the form of tears as he zigzagged through the trees and toward safety.

"This is Blaze," he said as they approached a beautiful ginger mare. Tied to a tree trunk, she stood tall and threw her head high in the air, as though nodding, when they reached her. "She's a good girl."

"She's stunning," Reese said as he hoisted her onto the saddle.

He mumbled a thank-you as she kept watch, looking for any movement other than branches being nudged around by the wind while he took up the reins. The rain had stopped, and lucky for them had not saturated the ground, which would make getting away on horseback faster.

Ignoring the thunder in between her temples, she sucked in a breath when Darren's arms closed around her from behind. Awareness skittered across her skin as he held tight to her, his chest against her back as he squeezed his thighs around Blaze, telling her to go.

She couldn't count how many times they'd ridden his horse Peanut, or how much teasing he'd endured for the name. It didn't matter that Darren had named the paint horse when he was ten. Peanut was stuck with the name, and so was Darren.

One hand wrapped around the saddle horn and the other holding the weapon, Reese kept her eyes on the trees. Since it was December, there were no leaves to hide behind in this area. The clouds shielded their eyes from the sun, but other than it obviously being daytime, she had no clue what time it was.

Had this been about robbery?

Her missing purse indicated that was a possibility, but did robbers kidnap people and stick around after getting their bounty? Maybe her purse was somewhere back in the old building. They'd gotten out of there so fast, she didn't think to search the place. Wouldn't a robber have knocked her on the head, stolen her handbag and hurried away? Instead, she was taken to a specific place, where several men had stuck around. There'd been no female voices, as best as she could recall. And then, somehow, Darren Pierce had arrived.

To spare herself the agony that thinking was causing, she pushed aside her thoughts. Besides, Blaze's canter was enough to scramble her brain.

Seeing him again reminded her of everything she'd had to give up to get out of Cider Creek. At eighteen, she hadn't realized how long the nights were about to become, or how lonely living by herself might be. Darren's uncle had offered her a chance to leave her life behind. Young and naive, she'd jumped at the opportunity to get away from her grandfather. He'd helped her with the transition and the two had become involved romantically, much to her later regret.

Darren stopped in front of a small, tidy barn big enough for a pair of horses, and then helped her down. Standing there, for a split second it was almost like she had gone back in time, and was in his family's barn, looking into those serious eyes. His irises were the most incredible shade of brown, surrounded by clear white rivers, framed by thick, almost black eyelashes. His curly hair was always in need of a haircut, his face was almost too hard, and there had been just enough scruff on his face to give her goose bumps when his skin had come in contact with hers as he feathered kisses on the nape of her neck.

Reese shoved away that unproductive memory. It had her wanting to grab a handful of shirt and tug until his lips met hers. She missed the way he looked at her when they used to stand this close. It was gone now, which was a good reminder they were no longer a couple. She'd shut that down when she took off, too young to realize the tug at her heart when she thought about him would last a decade.

Coincidence might have brought them together again, but the reunion was temporary at best. She needed to assess the damage and then figure out how to get home to Dallas. Cider Creek, actually, she corrected herself.

"How are your legs now?" Darren asked.

"I think I can manage with a little help," she said.

Darren nodded, then removed Blaze's tack and ushered her into a stall where there was hay and water waiting. When he turned around to wrap an arm around her, his face twisted, as if touching her brought on physical pain. Since this didn't seem like the right time to apologize for leaving town and then dating his uncle, she kept her lips closed. She knew Darren. He would never forget what happened or forgive her despite her reasons.

The house was log-cabin style but modern. Everything seemed new, from the pine beams to the granite countertops. The living room and kitchen were open-concept and the place had Darren's warm and comfortable feel to the decor.

Two steps in and she took note of two walkers, the kind for babies to run around in. There was a pair of pink swings off to one side around the granite island.

Was Darren married with kids?

"I'm sorry to intrude," Reese said to him. "I'll arrange transportation. I'm sure your family needs you."

"The twins are with their grandma and law enforcement will have questions for you," he said to her. She immediately screwed up her face, because his mother had passed away when they were teenagers from a rare and aggressive cancer.

"Your in-laws," she said as he helped her to the

brown leather couch. There was a flat-screen TV on top of the fireplace mantel.

"Something like that," he mumbled so low she could barely hear. He didn't look like he wanted to explain, so she left the subject alone. Instead, she glanced at his ring finger and was surprised when there was no band or tan line.

Shelving those details under the heading "no longer her business," she eased onto the soft leather.

"What can I get you? Water? A pillow? A blanket?" he asked, then checked his phone. "The law just arrived to the site."

"Do you mind asking them to look for my purse?" she asked. "I take it everywhere with me. And my phones. I'm lost without them." The work messages might be stacking up despite her competent assistant stepping up to cover.

"Is there someone you can call? Someone who can handle work for a few hours?" he asked, holding out his cell.

"I have someone, who I hope will be fine. But, seriously, who remembers anyone's number anymore?" she asked, a little embarrassed that she couldn't remember the number to her right-hand person.

"We can do an online search later," he suggested.

"Right," she said, blinking a couple of times, as though the movement could help with her nausea. Those systems weren't even connected. "You asked if I needed anything. Water would be nice." Her mouth was as dry as the year she licked a hundred stamps for

Christmas cards. She'd feared her tongue might stick to the roof of her mouth for the rest of her life.

He went to the kitchen and brought her back a glass of water. In a flash, she saw the same hungry look in his eyes from years ago.

Or maybe it wasn't there at all. It was possible she saw what she wanted instead of what was there.

DARREN CHIDED HIMSELF for letting his gaze linger a few seconds longer on Reese's delicate features. There was something decidedly fragile about her right now that brought out his protective instincts. All he could say in his defense was that he must be a glutton for punishment.

"I'll call the doctor," he said as he walked back to the kitchen. Distance was good. It helped him stay focused. He made the call to Dr. Stacie and got her voice mail. Darren had barely hit the end button on his cell when it rang. It was the good doctor herself.

"Everything okay with the babies?" Stacie Larson asked, sounding panicked. To be fair, his call had come out of the blue.

"The girls are fine," he quickly reassured her. "I have a friend who was hit in the head before possibly being robbed. Think you can swing by? It's after hours and the nearest hospital is—"

"Far," Stacie said. "I know."

"Do you mind doing me this favor?" he asked, figuring it would be easier not to move Reese again now that he had her on the couch. Plus, Stacie moved four miles away from him to help with the twins.

"Your house?" Stacie said after a heavy silence. He had no idea what the sudden attitude shift was about. Or did he? She was aunt to his twins and over-protective.

"Yes," he confirmed. "It's important to me or you know that I wouldn't ask."

Stacie let out a sharp breath.

"I'll leave now," she agreed before ending the call without warning.

He turned to Reese, who'd made herself comfortable on the couch, and said, "Help is on the way."

"Are you sure bringing a doctor here is a good idea?" she asked.

"The law will want to stop by and question you after checking out the equipment building," he explained as he retrieved a glass of water for himself.

"Can they do that at the hospital?" she asked.

"I guess so," he said. "Why? Are you uncomfortable here?"

"This is your family home," she said. "I feel like I'm intruding."

"You're not," he said, realizing he might not be rolling out the red carpet, but he didn't want to throw her out, either. He wasn't built that way. If someone needed a hand up, he couldn't turn his back. Call it the cowboy way, but it was ingrained in him. "I want you to stay."

"Won't your wife have an issue with me being here?" she asked. The question was fair given their history, he supposed.

"If you're talking about heightened teenage hor-

mones making us feel in love, that happened a long
time ago," he clarified. "We're grown adults now, I
have children and no residual feelings toward you."
The lie about his feelings tasted sour on his tongue
now that he heard the words out loud. For a split second, he'd convinced himself that he actually believed
it. Correcting it now didn't seem like the right play.
He fell back on defense, realizing he couldn't leave
it like that. "Which means that I'd like to help and no
one will question me about it."

Half a dozen emotions played out across her features before she settled on the one that he never could
quite read. All those years ago, he'd known she was
holding something back. All this time later, she didn't
seem any closer to letting him in on the secret.

"I appreciate your kindness, Darren," she said.
Hearing his name roll off her tongue wasn't helping
with those old unresolved feelings that were trying
to surface. Reese had sent him a text to let him know
she was leaving town and taking a job with his uncle.
She'd said the two of them should take a break and
figure out who they were without each other. The
next news he heard was the two started dating. Talk
about gutting an eighteen-year-old. He would have
warned her about the man, but it would have come off
as jealousy and his hurt pride wouldn't allow him to
contact her once she blew him off. He'd licked those
wounds for a solid year.

Darren told himself forgetting the hell he went
through because of her would be a bad idea. Keep-

ing the recollection near the surface would help him stay focused.

Besides, the twins would be back tomorrow and his normal life of diapers and everything pink would resume.

"It's settled then, right?" he asked. "You're staying for a while?"

"Yes," she said. "But the minute anything changes, you let me know."

Why did she always have her running shoes tucked next to the door? Or maybe a better question was, what had made her that way?

"Deal," he said, figuring this wasn't the time for questions even she most likely didn't have answers to. He bent down and picked up Iris and Ivy's favorite blanket. The feel of the silk lining in his hands connected him to the girls, and to the life he'd made long after his fool heart had been broken into pieces that never seemed to fit back together quite right again. There were too many jagged edges now that could cut through his chest if he breathed the wrong way.

"How well do you know the doctor?" she asked, sitting up. Her face twisted in pain with the move and her hand came up to her forehead, like she could somehow dull the ache by touching it.

"My daughters are her nieces," he replied. "But I have other questions right now."

She nodded as a look of dread washed over her. He'd seen the look before whenever he talked about the possibility of life after high school in Cider Creek.

"I've been trying to remember what happened and have been drawing a blank," she admitted.

"Do you know why you were near my property?" he asked.

"Nope," she sighed in a way that detailed her frustration. "I assumed they brought me here. Whoever *they* are."

"Any recent fights with anyone?" he asked. "Does anyone wish you harm?"

She caught his gaze and held it.

"If you're asking if I have enemies who would knock me out, abduct me and then hold me in a random building, then I couldn't say," she stated. "I hope I don't know anyone who is capable of this kind of cruelty."

He lowered his head when he said, "Sorry to hear about your grandfather."

"Don't be on my account," she countered. "You, of all people, should know Duncan Hayes and I weren't close."

"Still," he continued, "it's a loss."

Reese shrugged as she said, "I guess so."

When did she get so cold? Then again, their history suggested she'd been heartless since the end of high school. Did anyone really ever change?

## Chapter Three

Duncan Hayes was the reason Reese and her siblings couldn't get out of Cider Creek fast enough. The only hitch back then had been the thought of leaving Darren. At eighteen, she thought she was being smart about her life, putting her future before her heart. She'd looked up the statistics on successful marriages of high-school sweethearts. They weren't good. Plus, she didn't think she would be good at marriage, anyway.

Besides, sticking around Cider Creek was never an option for her. Darren had family to think about and their ranch needed him to stay on to survive.

"Why would someone bring me here?" she asked, suddenly wondering if this incident could somehow be tied back to him.

He shrugged.

"I haven't seen or heard from you in years," he pointed out. The slight edge to his tone suggested he didn't care for the tables being turned.

"I'm trying to look at this from every angle," she elaborated. "Please don't think I'm attacking you in any way."

Darren sat there for a long, thoughtful moment. He always got quiet when conflicting thoughts battled for control. "We're good."

No. They weren't. The two of them were anything but on good terms. Darren was being kind enough to help her despite their rocky past, and she appreciated him for his generosity. They'd left on bad terms all those years ago and the set to his jaw, along with those piercing eyes when he looked at her, told her where they stood. He was tolerating her because he lived by a code that said he helped anyone in need. Ranchers were always there for each other. Too bad her grandfather hadn't been there for his family in the way he had been for the community. Watching everyone admire the man who'd made everyone's lives miserable had been a tough pill to swallow. Folks in town revered Duncan, and the rest of the family had put up a believable front that they were a strong unit. Only those precious few who got close to her or one of her siblings learned the truth. Duncan was a piece of work. The first word that came to mind was *controlling*. The second would have gotten her mouth washed out with soap when she was little.

Anger burned through her chest. Why couldn't she block out her grandfather instead of the last few hours?

Darren's cell buzzed at around the same time the front door swung open. A look of hesitation crossed his features before he went for his phone. A blonde woman walked in the door as he studied the screen.

He glanced up, then nodded and hitched his free thumb toward Reese.

"I'm Dr. Larson," she said, making a straight line toward Reese. The doctor could best be described as pretty. She was also tiny, but there was nothing delicate about her mannerisms. Shoulders square and stiff, starched shirt tucked into neatly pressed navy slacks, everything about her said she was put-together and serious. Her hair was slicked back in a ponytail that fell past her shoulders. Powder-blue eyes and pink lipstick softened her look a couple of notches, making her seem more approachable.

"Reese Hayes," she said as she took the outstretched hand. "It's nice to meet you."

The good doctor glossed right over Reese's comment. Those blue eyes looked Reese up and down as if she was sizing her up for a coffin.

"Thank you for coming on such short notice," Darren said.

The quick nod and chilly reception gave Reese the impression these two were more than just friends.

"Tell me what happened and where it hurts," Dr. Larson said, setting her bag down on the floor as she perched on the edge of the solid oak coffee table. She kept one hand on the handle. A stethoscope hung around her neck. Black ballet flats peeked out of the bottom of her pant legs.

Reese explained what little she knew. She pointed out where it hurt the most.

"It looked like she took a blow to the back of her head, based on the blood in her hair," Darren said from across the room. When the doctor didn't respond, he looked up from his phone and said, "Stacie."

Reese couldn't help but wonder just how close Darren and Stacie were, even though it wasn't any of her business. Tell that to her brain, because it wanted to know the exact nature of their relationship. It didn't help when Darren joined them in the living room, choosing to sit next to Stacie so close that their thighs touched. While he didn't seem to think twice about it, a flash of emotion crossed behind Stacie's eyes.

There was a familiar air between the two of them, too. She didn't get the girlfriend-and-boyfriend vibe. Although, it would serve Reese right if he flaunted a beautiful, successful woman under her nose to remind her of what she'd lost when she'd left town—him.

"I noticed the blood," Stacie said dismissively as she flashed a small light she'd retrieved from her bag in Reese's eyes. The exam and questions that followed seemed routine, like she could perform it in her sleep.

When everything was put away, Stacie closed the bag. She leaned forward, elbows on her knees, and clasped her hands together. "I cleaned up the wound on your head. There's a pump knot with a little cut that should heal fine on its own without sutures. My biggest concern right now is your lapse in memory. It's not uncommon in the case of trauma to block out the events leading up to the incident. Unfortunately, there's no quick fix or guarantees. In some cases, the memories come back. In others, they're gone for good. The brain goes to great lengths to protect us from memories that might cause us additional pain."

"What about her headache?" Darren chimed in. "How long will that last?"

"I was getting to that," Stacie said. "You can take OTC medication as directed to alleviate your headaches. If they get worse, give me a call. I can write a prescription for something stronger even though I'd prefer not to for the next couple of days."

Reese wasn't much on taking pills. "I'll be fine with ibuprofen."

Stacie nodded. "Avoid alcohol and driving for a few days until you're feeling better again."

The alcohol was no problem, but the driving meant she couldn't get back to Dallas or her job any time soon unless she asked Darren for another favor or made a major request from her assistant who needed to be in the office.

"Okay," Reese agreed. She needed to come up with a plan to get home, preferably in the next couple of hours. She was still holding on to the hope her purse and cell phones would be found by the law. She could ask Darren as soon as Stacie left. Her keys were inside her handbag as well. She was at a loss without it.

Reese cracked a small smile. Here she was thinking about car keys when she didn't know where her vehicle was. It could be totaled or in a ditch somewhere at this point. Or both. Those details were still blank.

She might be putting too much stock in one option, but maybe the law could tell her where her vehicle was and in what condition.

"Other than that, rest," Stacie said with an emphasis on the last word. Her gaze narrowed the next time she opened her mouth to speak. "For the record…" Her lips clamped shut almost as fast as they'd opened. Had she thought better of speaking her mind? "Suffice it to say I'll be nearby if anything comes up."

Darren immediately stood up, bringing Stacie up with a hand on her elbow. "I'll walk you outside."

Reese would like to be a fly buzzing around for that conversation.

"There's no need," Stacie said as she bent down to pick up her bag. She gave Reese another up-and-down stare with ice in her eyes. "I know where the door is. I can show myself out."

Rather than tell the good doctor that she had nothing to worry about, Reese took the high road and thanked the woman. Stacie must feel threatened by Reese's presence. She wanted to say, "Believe me, honey, you have nothing to worry about." Darren would never move beyond the past and Reese had no right to ask him to despite her heartstrings being tugged by his presence.

Darren's stubborn streak was a mile long and he would never forgive her.

Darren walked behind Stacie as she cut across the lawn toward her vehicle. Part of him felt the need to protect Reese from Stacie, and the other part—the one that had been burned—said Reese was a grown woman capable of handling her own affairs.

"Hey, what just happened?"

Stacie whirled around on him, index finger up and

pointed like she was about to poke him in the chest. At least she wasn't ready to smack him with her medical bag. "What?"

"Come one. Don't play games," he countered. "Not even a Texas summer could melt the ice back there."

Stacie blew out a sharp breath that he was certain would freeze rain. "Is it wrong that I'm overprotective of my nieces?"

"It is when there's no reason to be," he said.

"Who is she then?" Stacie asked, moving her pointer finger toward the door.

"Someone I went to high school with a long time ago who ended up on my property, tied up in my equipment room," he replied.

She sucked in a deep breath. "Why? Who would do that to her?"

"Those are good questions but all I know for certain is that she was being held against her will," he confided.

"Oh," Stacie said.

"And now the law is out there looking for clues about who did that to her and why because she can't remember," he continued.

"I was off base, but that doesn't mean I wouldn't do it all over again if it meant protecting those babies," Stacie conceded. The bull-in-the-china-shop routine was starting to fade as some of the tension in her face muscles eased. "It's only been a year and—"

"What?" he interrupted. "You think I've somehow forgotten her?"

"Well, no, but—"

"I haven't," he said. "And I won't. But it has been a solid year and I will get back on the dating horse at some point."

"With *her*?" Stacie blurted out. A look of embarrassment flashed across her features.

"Does it matter?" he asked. "Someone will come along at some point. I'll be ready to kick-start that part of my life again."

Stacie stood quiet for a few moments. He could see this was hard on her. Him moving on was another reminder that her baby sister was gone. He didn't want to get into the details of just how complicated his relationship with his wife had become before the pregnancy, or the fact that he wasn't a hundred-percent certain the twins were biologically his. The guitar-player ex-boyfriend from Hazel's past might share their DNA.

"I guess not," Stacie admitted after another long pause. "You have a right to live your life. I do realize that."

"If I start falling down on my duties as a father, I hope you'll call me out," he said, knowing full well he would never do that to his girls. The statement was meant to placate their aunt.

"You can count on that," she said with a half smile. It was better than nothing.

"Good," he said. "Thanks again for coming out on such short notice."

"Call me if her condition worsens," Stacie said. "Every patient is different, but the vitals are strong on this one. My guess is that she'll be fine in a couple of days."

"That's good news," he said, then they said their goodbyes.

"You need to be careful with this one," Stacie warned as she got inside her sedan.

Rather than debate those words, or explain himself, he turned toward the house. "Drive safe."

Darren cut across the lawn as his cell buzzed again. He checked the screen about the same time he reached the door. After a quick scan of the message, he opened the door and stepped into the living room. "The sheriff is on his way."

"Any chance he found my personal belongings?" Reese asked as she immediately sat up.

"He didn't say one way or the other," Darren admitted. "Are you hungry?"

Reese crossed her arms over her chest. "That ibuprofen sounds good if you have any." Her body language tensed. The reason most likely had to do with Stacie.

"I do," he said. "Can you eat something first? It's not good to take on an empty stomach."

The way she scraped her teeth across her bottom lip told him she had questions but wasn't sure she should ask them. "I could probably eat a piece of toast if you have bread."

"What about a sandwich?" he asked as he moved toward the kitchen.

"Turkey?" she asked.

"Always," he said before stopping himself. Every

day after school, she'd had a turkey sandwich at his house. He made sure it was stocked since it had been her favorite, a habit that stuck to this day.

"I could try," she said, taking one of the throw pillows, then hugging it against her chest.

He fixed the sandwich and then brought it into the living room. Sitting next to her on the couch wouldn't be the smartest idea, so he took the leather chair instead.

"Something has been niggling at the back of my mind and I can't for the life of me figure out what it is," she said, picking up the sandwich. She took a bite and made a face.

"What just happened?" he asked.

"Nothing," she said, recovering almost as fast. "This is great."

"That's not what your face said a second ago," he argued. "Come on. I'm a big boy. Tell me what's wrong with the sandwich."

She shot him a look he recognized as an apology, then said, "Mayonnaise."

"You used to like it slathered on both sides," he insisted.

"I'm a mustard girl now," she said, then took another bite. "But don't even worry about it. I'm used to it now."

He moved to the kitchen, then brought over a paper towel and handed it over. "Do you want to wipe the mayo off?"

With effort, she chewed the bite then swallowed. "Yes, please."

After wiping off most of the spread, she polished off the sandwich in no time. He handed over ibuprofen and a refilled glass of water.

"Camree Lynn," she said with an ah-ha look on her face.

"What does she have to do with you being here?" he asked. Her best friend had disappeared off the face of the earth in tenth grade and never resurfaced.

## Chapter Four

The name had popped into Reese's mind out of nowhere. "I don't have any other details. Just her name but this feels important."

"Is it possible you found out information that led you here?" Darren asked.

She shrugged. "Anything is possible, I guess." Without her cell or purse, she only had her memory to rely on, and it wasn't very dependable at the moment.

"We have a name," he said.

That didn't mean much without additional context. *Useless* didn't begin to describe how she felt. Her head ached. The sandwich had eased some of her nausea. "It's awful to have a blank where there should be something, especially when that something might have been the reason for this." She held up her wrists to show the deep groves and red slashes.

"At least you're going to be fine," he said. "The rest can be figured out."

Reese took in a deep breath, then exhaled.

"Plus, the sheriff might find your belongings and

the law will be all over figuring out who did this to you," he said.

"I don't think I've ever been more scared in my life waking up to find that I'd been bound," she admitted before flashing her eyes at Darren. "Don't feel sorry for me."

He shot her a confused look.

"I'm not telling you any of this so you'll have sympathy," she clarified. Walking away in the manner in which she had, with a text instead of a person-to-person conversation, had been a jerk move.

"Not a problem on my side," he said so fast it almost made her head spin.

"Good." She was glad to clear it up. Looking around, she had so many questions about his life here. Would he answer any of them? Tell her that his life was none of her business? If he did, she wouldn't exactly blame him. Since trying to remember what happened and how she'd ended up here only gave her more of a headache, she decided it couldn't hurt to ask a few questions about his personal life. "How old are your babies?"

"Eighteen months," he responded, folding his hands together and staring at the carpet. It was the move he'd always done when he was uncertain about something. Why do it now?

"You don't know for sure?" she asked.

"What?" He looked up at her and one of his eyebrows shot up. "I know how old the girls are. Eighteen months, like I said."

"You did the thing you used to do…" she began and then stopped. "Never mind. That was a long time

ago. I don't know what I'm talking about anymore."
People changed after a decade, especially when they'd
only known each other as kids. Well, in high school,
anyway. Darren had a number of habits that were
probably different now that he was an adult, and
a father. *A father.* No matter how many times she
repeated the word in her head, it would still seem
strange. If the twins—girls, based on the explosion
of pink in the room—were a year and a half old, that
meant they were born when he was twenty-six years
old. Gestation took almost a year, so he would have
been twenty-five when they'd been conceived. Since
he wasn't wearing a wedding band, she assumed either he'd never been married, or he was divorced.

Darren would have done what he would have believed to be the "right" thing and proposed after a
pregnancy announcement. Ten years might have
passed, but she'd bet her savings account that Darren maintained his sense of honor. Call it cowboy
code or whatever, but it was the reason he still held
the door open for a woman, unless she asked him not
to. It was the reason he was helping her now. And it
was the reason he wouldn't ask her to leave unless
he knew she would be okay.

Helping her because he still had feelings after all
this time wasn't even a serious consideration.

When she looked over at him, he was studying her.

"I asked if you wanted more water," he said.

Her glass was empty. "Yes, please. If you don't
mind."

"It'll hopefully help with the headache," he said,

then stood and picked up the glass from the coffee table.

Darren moved into the kitchen. As he walked, she forced her gaze away from his strong, muscled back. He'd grown into his tall frame from the last time she'd seen him.

"Do you still work on the ranch?" she asked, needing to talk to work off some of her nerves at being back.

"The one my parents owned is mine now," he said as he refilled the glass. "Been that way since not long after you took off." The way he said those last few words sent daggers to the center of her chest. Without her cell, purse or keys, she was stranded here until the sheriff arrived. Making small talk didn't seem like the right plan. She should have known he wouldn't want to have anything to do with her outside of making sure she was safe. Conversation was probably asking too much.

Darren walked over and set the glass down on the table. His cell buzzed, indicating a text was coming through. He checked the screen. "The sheriff has been diverted on a call. He says it might be a while before he can get here."

"How far are we from Hayes Cattle?" she asked.

His face twisted. "Hour and a half, give or take. Why?"

"I've taken up enough of your time and generosity," she said, figuring he would want a break from all this so he could pick up his babies. "It might be for the best if I call to see if one of the hands can swing by and pick me up now that I think about it. If any of my things are found, we can always come back."

Going home reminded her of something she needed to do...but *what*?

"To be honest, you were found on my property and that makes this case my business," he countered after a thoughtful pause. "Unless you have a good reason, I'd appreciate you staying put. My children live in this home with me, and I need to know exactly what happened and how this case goes."

Reese caught his gaze and looked him dead in the eye. "You're sure that's what you want? Me in your house?"

The question caught him off guard based on the face he made. "You're here. I'm not asking you to leave."

"What if the sheriff takes a long time?" she continued. "Being in the same room with me after all these years can't possibly be high on your list of ways you'd like to spend a day."

"I didn't expect you to show up, but here you are and there are other rooms if I'm bothered," he said. "Time has passed and we've both moved on. This isn't high school anymore, Reese. We're grown adults who have pushed beyond a childish breakup." The manner in which he said those words made her feel otherwise. There was a tension in his jaw that only occurred when his coach had yelled at him during practice, or his father had dressed him down for being late to finish chores even when he had homework and tests to study for.

"If you're sure my being here doesn't bother you," she said, figuring he'd made good points about this being his home and where he was bringing up his children. He deserved to hear firsthand what the sheriff had to say. Plus, he'd been nothing but helpful so far, even if he had to force himself to be cordial.

"I'd tell you if I was," he said.

Would he, though? A small piece of her thought he might be as curious about her as she was about him. Then again, it had been a long day and she could be misreading his actions.

DARREN WAS DOING his best. Finding Reese on his property after all these years was one thing. Who would bring her here and why? As morbid as this sounded, even to him, why would someone hold her here instead of immediately killing her? More than one person had to be involved unless she'd come up on poachers who couldn't afford to let her go, but didn't have it in them to kill her. They might have been trying to figure out what to do with her, which may have included doing things *to* her. Anger made his blood run hot at the thought she could have been raped. There'd been more than one person present in the old equipment shed—a building that was going to be torn down the minute he received clearance from the sheriff. More of that anger boiled when he thought about his daughters being the ones inside there when they were older.

The building was dangerous. It had to go. He'd tear

it down with his bare hands if it meant no one would ever be bound inside those walls again.

Darren issued a sharp sigh as he caught Reese suppressing a yawn.

"The sheriff won't be here for a while," he said. "You're welcome to change out of those clothes into something more comfortable and grab a nap." He gave her a sympathetic look. "It doesn't sound as though you remember any of your clothing being removed at any point during your abduction." He used the last word for lack of a better term.

"A shower sounds like heaven," she said, shaking her head. "I would like very much to wash this dirt off me."

"I'm sure I have something around here that you could change into," he said, forcing an image of her naked and in the shower out of his thoughts. "Even if it's just a T-shirt and a long robe."

"Okay," she said.

It occurred to him that her clothing might be considered evidence. "I have a paper grocery-store bag to put your things in. The sheriff might need them for evidence."

"Right," she said on a heavy sigh. "That's a good point actually." She crossed her arms over her chest and rubbed them like she was suddenly cold. "I can't imagine what kind of monsters would do something like this to another human being. I'm not sure what happened, but..." Her voice trailed off.

"You might have gotten in the way of poachers," he said, trying to find a way to offer some reassurance. "You weren't physically assaulted, which is a good sign." Hearing those words come out of his own mouth made a knot tighten in his gut. The fact any woman had to worry about being attacked once she left her home tipped his blood to boiling. Having daughters made him even more aware of the dangers women faced, and the feeling he wouldn't always be there to protect them sickened him to no end.

What happened to Reese today was a harsh reminder of what could happen to any woman. A random occurrence would mean the danger was gone. Poachers would move on and move out.

"You might have had something to do with it," she said, dropping her gaze to the carpet. "I have so many questions about what happened and why." She rubbed her arms again. "It might have been unintended, but you saved me from…whatever it was those men planned to do with me. Thank you."

"You're welcome," he said. "I'm just relieved you're okay." *Okay* was a relative term. She was shaken up, which was understandable.

She nodded.

"How about that grocery bag and shower," she finally said, pushing up to standing. As she took a step, her leg gave. In one quick motion, Darren was by her side, catching her, keeping her from falling on her backside. "I'm fine." She righted herself quickly, pushing him away as she regained her balance. "It's all good. I probably sat too long. That's all. I'm better now."

He took a step back. "Okay." The other possibility was that she'd lost her balance from the head injury. Stacie had given the green light, told them that Reese was medically sound. She also said to call if he had any concerns.

Reese wiped her hands down her shirt and took a couple of steps. "See. All good here."

It didn't erase his concerns, but seeing her walk without falling was a good start. "I'm right here if you need an arm to hold on to."

"I got this," she said in a tone that reminded him of her independent streak. Reese had always been the silent observer. She was so quiet in a room, it had been easy to overlook her for most of their lives. Except that he'd noticed her in middle school before she grew into her looks…and she'd been beautiful. Still was, which bothered him more than he wanted to admit.

He stood there, waiting for the inevitable question.

"Which way to the bathroom?" she asked.

"Down this hallway," he said, pointing toward the guest area. "I'll grab a few things and meet you in the hallway outside the door. There are unused toothbrushes underneath the sink."

She nodded and left the room. After gathering a few supplies, he stood outside the bathroom door and knocked.

The door opened enough for him to slide the items into her hands.

"Take your time in there," he said. "If I hear from the sheriff, I'll let you know."

After receiving confirmation, he headed back into

the living room and grabbed his phone. A quick check of local news didn't reveal anything about the abduction.

He made a quick call to check on his daughters, and found out they were doing fine. As he held his phone, he looked at the wallpaper on his phone. The picture of his wife holding their newborn twins wasn't something he believed he'd ever replace. The girls were older now and their looks had changed so much. It might be time to update the photo.

A noise sounded from the hallway. Darren jumped to his feet and made a beeline for the bathroom door. He accidently stepped on Ivy's favorite rattle and almost face-planted. His reflexes were solid. A quick hand up to grab hold of the fireplace mantel saved him. The girls' belongings were strewn around the living room, but he liked seeing reminders of them everywhere, especially on nights they slept over at Stacie's, or at their grandparents'. Being poked in bare feet wasn't as heartwarming as he hopped around, cursing, but at least this time, he had his shoes on. Thank the stars.

"Everything good in there?" he asked, standing at the door.

"I'm all right, but your shower curtain might not survive," Reese said with a moan of what sounded like embarrassment.

"Mind if I open the door?" he asked.

"Give me a sec," she said. The naked image of her wasn't one he needed burned in his thoughts.

Another noise sounded in the living room, sending an ominous feeling rippling through him. "Hold on. I'll be right back."

## Chapter Five

Reese didn't like Darren's tone. She'd heard it before when there'd been trouble brewing. After what she'd been through today, it sent her pulse through the roof. Had the person who'd abducted her—and abduction was the only logical explanation, since there was no way she'd go with a stranger willingly—figured out where she was?

The thought had her racing to get dressed. Since her clothes were in a paper bag in the hallway, she shrugged into the oversized T-shirt and then the bathrobe. She kicked the shower curtain to one side to clear a path to the door, then reached for the door handle.

The door opened before she got to it.

She gasped, bringing her hand up to cover her mouth.

Darren took one look at her face and held his hands up, palms out, in the surrender position. "It's fine. A bird took a nosedive into the glass patio doors. They're reflective, so birds sometimes make the mistake of thinking they can fly right through."

"I thought maybe the guys found me here and were

coming for me," she admitted. A glance at the mirror as she walked past revealed a ghost-white reflection. She took in a couple of deep breaths to calm her nerves.

"Believe me," he said, "I was under the same impression."

"It's dangerous for me to be here," she pointed out. "You have a family, Darren. If anything happened to you or your girls because of me, I would—"

"You didn't bring this fight to my doorstep," he interrupted. "Someone else did and it's not your fault. Until we know who is behind this, I highly doubt we'll figure out why it happened. Unless by some miracle, you get your memory back."

This didn't seem like a good time to say he was, in fact, the last person she'd wanted to bump into in or near Cider Creek despite the growing part of her that was happy to see him. Even the tiny worry lines creasing his forehead made him look better than he had years ago. She doubted it worked like that for anyone else. Darren was different. Special.

"That may very well be true," she said, thinking he had a good point. "I could make sure that I'm seen somewhere else. Draw these jerks away from you and your girls instead of toward."

"Careful, Hayes," he said, then turned toward the living room. Out of the side of his mouth, he added, "I might actually think you've started caring about someone besides yourself."

Those words stung more than she wanted them to. Was there truth to them? She couldn't argue that she'd been in self-preservation mode at eighteen years old.

Living at Hayes Cattle had become hell thanks to her grandfather. Reese had watched her mother hang on to a life that didn't exist anymore. Why she'd stuck around the cattle ranch after her husband's death was something Reese might never understand.

The real reason her mother was calling everyone home was still a head-scratcher. Even more than that, all four of her brothers were making plans to upend their lives to move home or be around more. It was insanity and they'd lost their minds if they believed she would leave the city to return to a place that never quite felt like home to her in the first place. Then again, work jeans and overalls were the standard-issue clothing for the ranch. No high heels needed.

Camree Lynn had made all the difference. Reese's best friend had made living on the ranch survivable. The two had been inseparable by freshman year. Reese couldn't count the number of nights they'd stayed up, dreaming of shaking the dust of their little town off their feet and moving to a big city like Dallas, where people ate more sushi than steak. Fort Worth was where all the cowboys lived. Dallas had businesspeople and fashion designers. It had restaurants and bars.

Camree Lynn had been Reese's saving grace.

An involuntary shiver rocked her body thinking about the past, about her friend and her unsolved disappearance. There was always something niggling at the back of Reese's mind that she could never quite reach. It was almost as though she'd blocked out part of her memory. Trauma, she decided. She'd shut down back then, but pretended to be fine after overhearing

Duncan trying to convince her mother to send her to a "home for disturbed children," as he'd put it. Reese learned a valuable lesson in whom she could trust. Her mother put up an argument, but Duncan usually got what he wanted in the end. But not that time.

Immersing herself in her job—a job she loved despite the long hours and hard work—was so much better than thinking about Cider Creek. Reese realized she remembered her mother calling everyone home.

"You coming?" Darren's voice startled her out of her reverie. There was a cold quality to it that she probably deserved, but didn't like. Since she couldn't remember why she'd shown up in the first place, how she got here or who was after her, trying to leave didn't make a whole lot of sense. Selfishly, she wanted to stay, if only to be in the presence of someone who actually cared if she lived or died. Of course, her family did. Putting them in danger didn't seem like the best of ideas. When it came to no-win situations, this one took the cake and ate it, too.

"My mom wants us all home." She tightened the belt on her robe and then followed the voice into the kitchen area, stepping over baby paraphernalia along the way.

"Is that why you're here?" he asked.

"Has to be part of the reason but something tells me there's more," she said.

He nodded.

"What's it like?" she asked as he leaned a slender hip against the granite countertop.

He shot her a confused look.

"Being a father?" she asked.

"Scary," he said almost instantly. The quick response was honest. It had been his blink reaction to the question. "Great. The best thing to ever have happened to me. Tiring. Roll every intense emotion you've ever had into a ball, and there you go."

She smiled. His face lit up even when he talked about the tiring part.

"What about you?" he asked. "You change your mind about ever wanting kids?"

"Me?" She twisted up her face. "No. I couldn't do that to a child."

"What? You'd be a good mother," he said.

"Because I had such an amazing example?" she countered.

"Your mom is a sweetheart," he said without hesitation. He would know better than her now, considering she hadn't set foot in Cider Creek in ten years. Of course, she texted with her mother and made time for the occasional phone call. She sent flowers on Mother's Day and Christmas.

"She's a pushover. She let my grandfather walk all over her while she lived in the shadow of a marriage that didn't exist," she said, almost wishing she could take the words back. They sounded harsher when she spoke them out loud.

Darren stood there for a long moment, looking deep in thought. "Doing what's right for others even if it hurts you isn't being weak."

She shook her head. "I wasn't saying she was…"

Actually, she was doing just that whether she wanted to acknowledge it or not.

"Speaking of family," Darren said through clenched teeth, "how's my uncle?"

Reese didn't mean to suck in a breath even though she did. "I wouldn't know. I haven't worked for him in five years."

"You mean the two of you aren't dating anymore?"

Taking in a slow breath did little to stem the pain from what felt like daggers straight to her heart. The relationship with his uncle hadn't been something she'd planned. Looking back, the man knew what he was doing, though. He'd seduced her in a matter of months, made her believe she was special and then laughed when she'd confronted him about the others he'd been seducing, too. He'd casually said there'd been no mention of commitment. True enough, the words had never been spoken, only assumed. At least, on her part. And he'd never explicitly said he was seeing other people, not even in so many words. All those late nights at the office, when he'd sent her home alone with work, hadn't registered as him cheating. Then again, he'd made a good point. He couldn't cheat on a relationship that didn't exist in the first place. "No. We aren't."

Rather than stand there and continue this conversation, she moved to the patio doors. Tears welled in her eyes as she realized just how much she'd hurt Darren by leaving and how foolish she'd been to believe a much older, more experienced man when he said words she never would believe from someone her own age. Just like she'd always suspected, true love equaled devastation and misery. To find proof, all she had to do was take a look in Darren's eyes.

DARREN FIXED A pot of coffee. Since he'd already checked on the babies, there wasn't much else he could do there. Being busy had become a way of life since the pregnancy, forget once the twins were born. Six months was too young to lose their mother and he'd had no idea how he was going to bring up the babies on his own. Then, Stacie had shown up, ready and willing to pitch in. His in-laws came next and he started to think he might actually pull this whole thing off and bring up healthy young women.

Seeing Reese again reminded him of what could happen if he messed up the job.

Kids needed parents. Preferably both, even if they lived under separate roofs, which was where he and his wife had been headed before the twins had been conceived.

Darren shook off the memories. Thinking about the past was about as productive as trying to milk a bee. Besides, walking down memory lane made him relive all the hurt he'd experienced when Reese had walked out. How foolish had he been at eighteen to believe he'd found the love of his life?

Right now, his heart only had room for two girls— Ivy and Iris.

Reese didn't turn to look at him. "She likes you," she finally said after staring out the doors for a few minutes.

"We're family," he said, reaching for a mug.

"No," she said without hesitation. "She *likes* you."

"Stacie?" he asked. "She's just concerned about the twins, trying to make sure I'm doing a good enough job now that her sister is gone."

"I'm sorry," Reese said quietly. "It must be hard to lose the love of your life and the person you decided to build a family with."

Darren didn't know how to respond, considering he had lost the love of his life once. She should have been the mother of his children, but wasn't. The smart thing to do would be to keep a safe distance between him and Reese, in case any of those old feelings decided to rear their ugly heads and come back to bite him in the backside.

"It's never easy to lose someone," he said, deciding not to go into more detail than that. First loves had a way of gutting a person, making it hard to go all-in with the next one no matter how great they might be. What he'd felt for Hazel was good. He'd loved her as much as he could love anyone after having his heart stomped on. None of which was Hazel's fault. She'd loved him in her own way, too.

"I can't imagine," she said, but an emotion crossed her features that said she had some idea. Was it his uncle that she missed?

Darren couldn't let himself go there without anger boiling. Since getting mad wouldn't change the past, he shifted focus. Besides, anger never fixed anything. In fact, it usually led to someone popping off at the mouth and making the situation a whole lot worse.

"I'll check on the sheriff," he said, figuring the abduction was a whole lot safer subject. He retrieved his cell phone and checked the screen. He'd missed two calls from Stacie. "I need to make a call."

Reese nodded.

"Coffee is ready if you'd like a cup," he said. "Mugs are on the counter."

Receiving two calls from Stacie back-to-back set his nerves on edge. He walked over to the front window and returned the call.

"Is everything all right with the girls?" he immediately asked, concerned Stacie had information his former in-laws didn't want to deliver. He'd checked on them a little while ago but little kids were unpredictable and he'd learned the hard way were a danger to themselves half the time.

"Yes," Stacie said. "Sorry. Didn't mean to worry you. I just didn't like the way we left things earlier and wanted to make sure everything was okay between us."

Darren let out a sigh of relief.

"We're good," he said, trying to will his racing pulse to calm the hell down.

"Are you sure?" she asked. There was a quality to her voice that was different. Jealous? Was Reese right about Stacie wishing there could be more between them? He'd met her first, before Hazel. They'd gone out once but nothing happened because they'd gone to the restaurant where her sister worked as a waitress. As it turned out, Stacie was the practical sister. She studied and not much else. They'd run out of things to say to each other before the appetizers arrived. Hazel was the untamed sister. She was like a tornado who blew threw his life, turning everything upside down. Conversation with her had been easy. Sex had been fiery, but he found out later that there wasn't as much love between them as there was friendship. It was what he missed about her most despite her betrayal.

Hazel had asked her sister for his number, she'd given it, so he'd assumed she'd been just as bored on their date as he'd been. "I'd tell you if we weren't."

"How is she?" Stacie asked, not mentioning Reese by name. He'd pinned the situation right. He'd heard jealousy in her tone. Since he was going to start dating at some point, he needed to find a nice way to tell her that anything besides friendship was out of the question. At least it was on his side.

"Better," he said.

"Does she remember anything else?" Stacie asked. He figured she wanted Reese out of his home as fast as possible. The quicker she remembered, the faster she would leave.

"Nope," he admitted. Reese's words came crashing into him. Did Stacie want to step into her dead sister's shoes?

## Chapter Six

Reese couldn't help but listen to the phone call between Darren and Stacie. It had to be the doctor, based on his answers.

The woman, no doubt, wanted Reese as far away from Darren as possible. Did she not realize how much disdain Darren had for Reese? After grabbing a fresh cup of coffee, Reese headed into the living room. She noticed a small picture on the fireplace mantel of a woman holding the twins. They couldn't have been more than a few days old. The woman was beautiful. The resemblance to her sister was clear, even though the two looked like opposites. Stacie was put-together. Everything about her was neat, from her blown-out hair to her neatly trimmed nails. The woman in the picture had big bright eyes and wild hair. She was smiling but there was a sadness in her eyes. Reese couldn't help but wonder what had happened to her.

Her heart went out to the babies, who would grow up without their mother. Based on all the baby supplies, Darren was a good provider. Based on her own experience, unconditional love and acceptance was all she'd needed growing up.

At the ranch, reminders of her father had been everywhere even though no one talked about him. Had it been too painful for her mother? Seeing Darren as a single father, and how hard that must be, was opening her eyes to what her mother might have gone through.

Kids weren't something Reese had ever wanted. She wasn't one of those girls who sat around watching future brides say yes to a dress. She'd never flipped through bridal magazines, not even if that was the only option while sitting in a waiting room. And she'd never been one to fantasize about what her own wedding might look like someday. But she sure as hell didn't expect someone to cheat.

As a kid, she wondered if there was something wrong with her. Camree Lynn had teased Reese about her lack of interest in marriage and family a few times. Her friend used to say that Reese would change her mind when she found the right person. As much as she'd been infatuated with Matias Ossian, Darren's uncle, love had never been part of the equation. But there was an even bigger problem. Reese had no interest in finding the kind of love she assumed her mother had with Reese's father. The kind that had doomed her mother to a lifetime of pain and heartache. For what? A few good years?

No thanks.

"I have to go, but I'll call you if anything changes," Darren said as Reese tuned back into his conversation with Stacie. Reese couldn't help but wonder if Darren had loved his wife in the all-consuming way people described. There'd been a distance in his eyes earlier that made her want to ask questions. The answers were none of her business, so she kept her mouth shut.

Darren studied his screen. "Sheriff is on his way."

"Oh, good," she said. "It'll be nice to wrap this up so I can get out of your hair."

Those words seemed the equivalent of a slap in the face to Darren. He opened his mouth to speak and then clamped it shut.

"I was just thinking it would be nice for all of this mess to be cleared up so you can get back to your family," she said. "The longer those jerks are out there, the more time you'll miss out on with your twins."

Again, he started to speak and then stopped himself.

"I'm actually not trying to offend you," she said by way of defense.

"Didn't think you were," he responded. "If I wanted to, I could send you somewhere else and get on with my life after giving my statement to the sheriff."

Well, this was going nowhere fast. Being without her phones made her jumpy. She couldn't fathom how many messages would be waiting when she finally checked in.

The sound of gravel crunching underneath tires drew their attention toward the front window. Reese walked over and peeked through the blinds.

"He's here," she said.

Darren joined her. "You're about to meet Sheriff Red Courtright."

"Sounds like a good ol' Southern boy," she said,

wishing she was back in Dallas, where she would be giving a statement to the police.

Red Courtright looked the part. He was tall and slim, and in head-to-toe khaki-colored clothing. He was wearing a cowboy hat that was nearly blown off and carried away in the wind. His belt buckle was huge and he had on boots. Exactly the picture someone would get in their mind when they pictured a small-town sheriff.

Darren opened the door as the sheriff's boots hit the porch. "Come on in, Sheriff."

Red Courtright nodded as his gaze shifted from Darren to her and back. He tipped his hat and said, "Ma'am."

Once inside, the trio exchanged handshakes. Reese introduced herself as she studied the middle-aged man who had remnants of red in his now-light hair. His front teeth were donkey-sized, and up close she could see a dotting of freckles on overly tanned skin.

"I'm afraid I have bad news," he said.

Darren motioned toward the kitchen table that had three chairs and two highchairs tucked around it. "What did you find out?"

"Your equipment building burned," the sheriff informed.

Darren smacked the table with his flat palm. "What the hell?"

"It burned to the ground before the law or volunteer firefighters could save anything," the sheriff continued.

"I thought they were already there collecting evidence," Reese said.

The sheriff shook his head. "My mistake."

"I'm guessing that means any evidence or DNA went up in flames, as well," Reese stated. It was brilliant when she really thought about it. There would be no trace left behind of the person or persons who'd abducted her, leaving the trail cold unless her vehicle or a witnessed showed up.

"Afraid so," the sheriff said.

"And the call that you mentioned?" Darren asked. "Was it possible that was made to draw you away from the scene of the crime?"

"It's looking that way," the sheriff said, shaking his head. "We can't trace the call back to a name." His fisted hand smacked the table. "Which means we'll put even more resources on this thing to find out who did this to you." His gaze shifted to Reese. "Mark my words, the perp will be behind bars soon."

"I appreciate it, Sheriff," she said. This area most likely didn't see the kind of crimes common in a big city like Dallas. Another reason to get home as soon as possible. Dallas PD would be more equipped to handle criminals in her opinion. She would point that out but figured it wouldn't make her popular with the sheriff. Since she needed him to be on her side, she decided not to comment on his inefficiency. "Was anything recovered in the area? Like my cell phones or handbag?"

He shook his head.

"We have Reese's clothing," Darren offered. He retrieved the paper bag and handed it over to the sheriff.

It didn't mean the other items were lost forever, considering she had no idea when she'd last had them on her person.

"We'll run these through forensics to see if we pick up any fibers," the sheriff said, then put up a hand like he was stopping traffic. "Before you get any ideas, I send these off to be analyzed and it'll take time for anything to come back. The real world isn't anything like what you see on those TV shows, where someone makes a call or pulls a favor. Investigations take time and I plan to be thorough."

"What about my car?" she continued, picking up the thread after nodding.

"There hasn't been an abandoned vehicle found," he admitted. "I'll need the make and model so we know exactly what we're looking for."

"I drive a teal Lexus," she said. "It's the smallest sport utility." From the corner of her eye, she saw Darren stiffen. She wanted to point out that she hadn't used a dime of family money for the purchase and it was already three years old by the time she bought it. Her body tensed as a reaction to him.

Reese reminded herself to breathe.

"NX 200t?" the sheriff asked.

"Yes, sir," she responded with a little more vigor than was probably necessary.

He paused long enough to shoot off a text. Then, he held up his phone. "Word is spreading as we speak. If your vehicle is in the area, we'll find it."

If she had her cell, she could put in a call to her landlord and find out if it was parked in her spot by some strange circumstance. No one in her building seemed eager to get to know one another, so it wasn't like she had any friends or could call one of her neighbors to check for her.

The thought stopped her in her tracks. How long had she been a resident? Four years now? And she didn't know anyone she could call? The thought made city living sound far less appealing when she thought about it like that. Then again, with the last name Hayes in a town like Cider Creek, small communities could be suffocating.

DARREN LEANED ACROSS the table and folded his hands. Not only had a crime occurred on his property, but he'd also been hit with a fire. It was too late to put up surveillance equipment. He was cursing himself for not thinking of it sooner. No one in their right mind would return to the scene of a crime when deputies and the sheriff were sure to be there.

Then again, this bastard had drawn law enforcement away. Poachers came here for white-tailed deer, desert bighorn sheep and the like. The illegal hunters were smart and they would think to cover their tracks. If they worked this area enough, they would know what kind of law enforcement they were working with as well. Were they too easy of an answer, though?

They could have scared Reese away without going through the motions of tying up her hands and feet. As a counterpoint, they wouldn't appreciate having a witness running around who could describe them or offer information on their whereabouts. She might have popped off at the mouth, or one of them might have recognized her as a Hayes and decided to try to cash in. He was just running through random ideas here, hoping something sounded right. A few things didn't add up. Like why would she have been on his property in the first place. She wouldn't be there for the fun of it.

"Has any member of the Hayes family been in contact with your office?" he asked the sheriff.

Sheriff Courtright's eyebrows shot up. It didn't take but a few seconds for him to figure out the implication Darren was making.

"As in reporting a ransom demand?" the sheriff asked.

"Yes," he said. "What if the persons who abducted Reese intended to ask the family for money?"

The Hayes last name seemed to finally register. His eyes widened and he got a look of recognition on his face.

"You're of *the* Hayes family of Hayes Cattle," the sheriff said to Reese. "You should have mentioned that before. I'd like to offer my sincerest condolences about your grandfather. Duncan Hayes was a good man."

"Yes." Reese looked like she forced a small smile. "Thank you." It also appeared as if it was taking everything inside her not to make a comment about the kind of man her grandfather really was. It must be eating her up inside to be told the man was such a good person when she knew the opposite was true at home.

"No, no one from the family has made a call to my office," he said.

Darren had had an insider's view to the family dynamic. Reese was the baby of the family. Everyone left before she came of age. Did she feel abandoned by her siblings? She must have on some level.

He hoped the twins stayed close throughout life. Their grandparents were older. They had Stacie if anything happened to him. But mostly, they had each other. They'd held hands the second they were placed next to each other. The image had melted his heart. Nothing else mattered—the second he laid eyes on those tiny angels, his heart had gone all in.

"With Mr. Hayes's death, I'm surprised it's taken this long for the vultures to come out if that was the original plan," the sheriff stated. It looked like he'd made up his mind about what happened already. "My office will do everything in its power to bring these men to justice before it happens again. If I were you, I'd be careful from now on until these perps are under lock and key. If they tried once, there's nothing stopping them from trying again."

"Are you certain that's what we're dealing with here?" Reese asked. She tilted her head to one side, like she used to do when she disagreed with someone but didn't want to call them out on it.

"It's a theory that makes sense," he responded.

She gave a slight nod, which told Darren she realized the sheriff had made up his mind at this point, and his idea was far-fetched. Arguing wouldn't do any good. In fact, he went so far as to tuck his cell inside his front pocket.

"I've got a lot of work to do on my end," he said.

"Thank you for your statement. Is there a way I can reach you in case I have follow-up questions?"

"I don't have my cell," Reese admitted, looking a little more than flabbergasted that the sheriff was ready to walk out the front door.

"You can reach her through me for now," Darren said, figuring the two of them were going to be joined at the hip over the next few hours, anyway. Possibly more. The thought should have repulsed him, or at the very least make him hot under the collar. With her here, he had a better chance of finding out what really happened so he could ensure it never happened again.

"Well, all right," the sheriff said before nodding toward Reese. Was he incompetent? Red Courtright didn't come across as the brightest bulb in the bunch. "If you'll excuse me. I have work to do."

Reese nodded and thanked the sheriff for his time. Her words came out almost robotic, but the sheriff didn't appear to catch on. His grin was almost ear-to-ear before his face turned serious and he offered more sympathy for her loss.

Darren walked the sheriff outside, and then returned to the table.

"It's quick and convenient," Reese said, then added, "I'll give him that much."

"Shouldn't be too difficult to prove him wrong," Darren said.

"What am I supposed to do in the meantime?" she asked, her tone more defiant than defeated, even though he detected both. He'd always loved her quiet confidence.

"Stick around here," he said, wondering if it was a good idea. There was no other choice if they wanted to get to the bottom of this thing. Trusting the sheriff seemed like the quickest way for Reese to end up abducted again. This time, the bastards would be more prepared.

Were they watching his house right now?

# Chapter Seven

Reese blew out a breath that depleted all the air she had in her lungs. She gave herself a moment of self-pity, but she'd learned a long time ago not to wallow there.

Taking in a deep breath, she decided to regroup.

"I can tell we're not working with a whole lot upstairs when it comes to the sheriff," she finally said to Darren, pulling the straps of her robe tighter. Granted, she might have on a long T-shirt underneath, but she had no plans to give any sort of peepshow.

"Believe me, I noticed, too," he said. "There's a decent deputy we can call who I've worked with before when tracking poachers."

"Except now that the high-profile name of Hayes is involved, I imagine the sheriff will want to run the show," she countered. Red Courtright might not have the highest IQ, and that was just a guess on her part, but he had to be savvy to have been elected to this job. Savvy or connected to someone prominent in the community. Hell, it could have been her grandfather who'd helped the man get elected for all she knew.

"That's a fair point," Darren conceded. "Reaching out might put my deputy in a bad position, so I'll table the thought for now."

"Sounds like the best course of action," she said, realizing she'd go stir-crazy if she sat here much longer and did nothing. Her friend's name kept coming full circle in Reese's thoughts. "I keep thinking about Camree Lynn."

She looked over at Darren, who sat a little straighter at the mention of her.

"Do you want to talk about her?" he asked. No one liked to say her name too loudly after she'd gone missing. The sheriff back then decided she was a runaway based on her journals, where she said she couldn't wait to get far away from Cider Creek.

"We can," Reese said, wondering if there could be a connection. "To your point, she disappeared a long time ago."

"You were her best friend," he pointed out, not that he needed to. It had been common knowledge.

"Which is why I know she didn't run away," she said. "She would have contacted me back then to let me know a plan so I could go with her. If anyone was going to run away, it would have been me."

"The sheriff at the time collected evidence from your text messages, your laptop and, if memory serves, your journal," he said.

Having someone dig into her personal thoughts was the worst kind of awful for a teenager. Since Duncan Hayes had been an "upstanding" citizen, the sheriff had returned her personal items to him. He'd made no secret of reading every page, and all the frustration she'd vented about him came to light. She'd been mortified. But it served him right on some level since he was the one who'd forced her to turn over the items in the first place in the name of cooperation.

"That's right," she said. "It gave my grandfather an eyeful."

"Your mother intervened," he pointed out.

"As best as she could," Reese stated. "There was only so much anyone could do when it came to Duncan Hayes. Every time someone speaks his name with reverence, I want to roll my eyes." It was probably a jerk move to hate him now that he was dead, but she had a long history of not liking the man, and he'd given her every reason to.

"He was bigger than the room," Darren agreed. "Used to scare the living daylights out of me, threatening to take me out back behind the barn and whip me if I ever laid a hand on you."

"It almost sounds noble when you put it like that," she said, "but he was only ever worried about me or my sister Liz coming home knocked up. His concern had everything to do with keeping up appearances. He didn't care if I ruined my life one way or the other as long as he came out smelling like a rose."

"That's probably true," he admitted. "It's probably parenting that's making me soft now, but I'd like to believe he cared about you and that had something to do with his reasoning."

"Did you know Rory has a daughter?" Reese asked.

"Your brother? When?" Darren asked.

"Liv is almost thirteen years old," Reese said. She heard the hint of pride in her own voice even though she'd never met Liv face-to-face.

"How did that happen?" he asked before putting a hand up to stop her from answering and, therefore, stating the obvious. "I *know* how it happened. How is it that no one knew?"

"Duncan Hayes ran Rory off the second he found out him and his old girlfriend got pregnant," she informed him. More proof that her grandfather had only cared about his own image. "My brother hid his child from the family all these years after Duncan practically forced him out of town at eighteen and Rory was too embarrassed to tell anyone until recently."

"There goes my hope your grandfather couldn't be all bad," he said.

"Believe me when I say that I wish it wasn't true," she said. "But those are the facts and we never spoke about it to anyone."

"What happened to Rory and his daughter?" he asked.

"My brother started a successful construction company and brought his daughter up on his own after his girlfriend decided being a young mother was too hard," she said. The news had come across in a group text and, rather than come home, Reese had called her brother to get the details. Rory had practically begged her to come back to visit so she could meet Liv. Was that the real reason she was in Cider Creek? "Liv sounds like a real sweetheart. A firecracker, but a sweetie nonetheless."

"Sounds like I need to call him for parenting advice," Darren said.

"You seem like you're doing all right so far," she said, hearing the hint of pride in her own voice.

Darren didn't look so confident in his abilities. "I've been able to get the hang of changing diapers and wiping more behinds than I ever wanted to see and, believe me, I'm exhausted. More than during any calving season I've ever experienced. I've rocked each one of the girls through their colicky phase and stressed over their first colds and fevers. The thing is, I feel like this might actually be the easy part. Like, it only gets harder from here."

"You're probably just remembering all the trouble you used to get into as a teenager," she said with a small smile. "You weren't a bad boy, but you liked to play pranks and generally give teachers a run for their money."

"That's exactly what I'm talking about," he said with wide eyes, like she'd just caught on to something. "There's probably going to be some karmic retribution for all my past sins."

She swatted a hand at him. "You did things but it's not like you were a criminal. You were actually a good kid."

"I doubt Coach Waterston would agree with that statement," he countered.

Darren had tucked one of those fake blood capsules people use at Halloween into the man's favorite ball cap. The baseball coach had a habit of hitting himself with the flat of his palm on top of his head before he ripped into someone, and that someone was usually Darren.

"To be fair, you got kicked off the team for that one," she said. "You paid your dues by not being allowed to try out for the baseball team ever again."

"If that was the only prank I ever played, I wouldn't be worried," he said.

"I guess you were a handful back then," she said. "But you calmed down a lot when we were together."

"You finally gave me a reason to stay out of detention," he said. "You were never there."

"Because I never spoke to anyone, except you," she pointed out. "I kept my head down and did my work. I did everything I could to deflect attention rather than draw it to me."

"You were always quiet, but it got worse after Camree Lynn disappeared," he remembered.

"That's what happens when your best friend goes missing and no one believes you when you say she wouldn't run away," she said.

"I get the part about reading her journal and finding out how badly she wanted to leave Cider Creek, but surely that wasn't all they had to go on," he said.

"No," she said. "There was more. She had been fighting a lot with her parents, who were getting divorced. The whole situation shook Camree Lynn up pretty badly. She threatened to run away a couple of times, but I know for a fact she was only making those threats to get attention. She told me so herself because she decided her parents might try to work things out if they believed the divorce was affecting her badly."

"Sounds like Camree Lynn to think something like that," he mused.

"Her parents were too far gone to bring their marriage back," Reese said. "They sat her down and told her as much and I'm pretty certain she was talking to guys she shouldn't have been in chat rooms even though no evidence was found."

"A troubled teen who was known to threaten to run away could have made for an easy mark for a creep," he said.

"My thoughts exactly," she agreed. "But the sheriff didn't think so. Neither did her parents. They got it inside their heads their daughter was making a play for their attention and would come home within twenty-four hours."

"I remember the case," he said. "Camree Lynn never came back to school. A body was never found."

"Because they didn't look for one," she quipped. "It's hard to find someone when you don't even bother to search for them."

"Even teachers believed she ran away, from what I remember," he said. "They were overheard talking about her in the teacher's lounge."

"What if she didn't?"

MUCH MORE OF this talk and Darren would go pick up his twins and never let them leave his sight again. Like he said before, as hard as this stage was, he feared this was going to be the easy part of bringing up children.

"You mentioned her before," he said to Reese.

"She was on my mind," she admitted.

"There could be other explanations than you thinking you'd found her trail," he said.

"How did you even know that I was thinking that?" she asked.

He shrugged, not really wanting to recall all those little details about her that he'd been trying to shut out of his thoughts for a decade. "But it makes sense that you would be returning home at some point because of your grandfather's death. Have you been back since he passed?"

She shook her head and then twisted her fingers together. "There hasn't been a reason to."

"Family," he said. Although, she'd made it clear that family wasn't exactly a priority for her.

"We've been spread out until recently," she said. "My sister Liz is probably the last person who would come home."

"Do you talk to them on a regular basis?" he asked.

"No," she admitted. "Pretty much all I do in Dallas is work."

"Sounds about right," he said.

"What's that supposed to mean?"

"Believe it or not, I wasn't trying to offend you," he insisted. "I was all about work until the girls came along."

Reese released a slow breath and then locked gazes with him. He wasn't ready for the gut punch that came with meeting her eye-to-eye.

"You look different," she said. "Good."

"I'm the same person, Reese."

"No," she argued. "You seem a lot more settled now."

"Kids have a way to doing that to a person," he snapped, figuring he could be insulted out there, but didn't have to put up with it in his own home.

"I didn't mean it in a bad way," she replied. "It's good, actually. I mean, when we were young, you had a restless quality. Like you were always searching for something to fill... I don't know—a void. Now, you have a confident air."

"Funny, bringing up the girls makes me feel like I have no idea what I'm doing in life or otherwise," he said.

"I guess you just seem comfortable with not knowing everything," she said. "Like, you know you'll figure it out along the way."

"What choice do I have?" His girls were the reason. And Reese was right, he would move heaven and earth to make sure he found answers to every question that pertained to them.

"Not everyone is as good a father as you are, Darren."

"You haven't even seen me with my daughters yet," he said. "How can you make a statement like that?" Why should he care so much that Reese Hayes seemed awestruck with any aspect of his life?

She shook her head. "I don't have to. It's in your eyes. It's in your determination when you talk about them. It's easy to see how much you love them and how devoted you are to them."

He hoped it was enough because there was no rule book when it came to parenting. One would think twins would have the same needs, but Ivy had an independent streak a mile long, whereas Iris was content to be with her sister all the time. He was going have his work cut out for him later in trying to make sure Iris understood Ivy's independence wasn't a rejection. When Ivy was tired at the end of a long day, her sister's presence comforted her the most.

"I appreciate your kindness," he said to Reese. But it was a little too early to pat himself on the back in the parenting department. "It means a lot. But this whole game is a crapshoot and it feels like any misstep could damage these things that I love more than life itself."

The jury was out on whether or not he would be a good dad after going the distance with his girls. He couldn't imagine the horror Camree Lynn's parents must have endured at losing their daughter at such a young age. It was against the natural order for a child to die before the parents.

Speaking of disappearances, he had an idea.

## Chapter Eight

"Since it's likely you were coming home at the time of the abduction, for lack of a better word, maybe you were making a pit stop first. Something about Camree Lynn's disappearance."

Darren had a point.

"What do you suggest we do?" she asked.

"Look for another disappearance. Something recent and something nearby," he continued. He held up a finger, then disappeared into what she assumed was the master bedroom.

Reese refilled her coffee mug and moved to the kitchen table as Darren returned with a laptop tucked underneath his arm.

"I do most of my paperwork while in bed after the girls go to sleep," he explained, but it was unnecessary. How he handled his business was up to him. She remembered from growing up on a cattle ranch how much paperwork was involved. Folks had several misconceptions about cattle ranching and the first one was that ranchers spent all their time herding cattle. There was far more tagging, tracking and recording than anyone realized. Another was that ranchers were all wealthy. Ranching was hard work and most barely kept their heads above water.

Duncan Hayes might have been a son of a bitch, but he'd been a keen businessman. His cold heart was good for something.

"I like the idea of looking for a connection," she said.

"We'd be searching for a serial abductor," he explained.

"Would so much time elapse in between, though?" she asked. "How could that be the same person if they just now struck again?"

"We might be looking for someone who moves around a lot for their job or travels. They might have fixated on Camree Lynn for one reason or another, but taking someone so close to home would draw a lot of unwanted attention," he said. "The person would wait a long time before striking here again."

"If at all." Reese took in a deep breath. "Sounds logical." All those old feelings of helplessness surfaced as she thought about her former best friend's disappearance. It was funny how kids always blamed themselves for things they have no control over. "I thought if I'd asked her to sleep over that weekend, she might still be alive because she would have been with me instead."

"If someone targeted her, they would have waited for another opportunity. It wouldn't have made a hill-of-beans difference," he quickly countered. His reassurance meant more to her than he could ever know.

Darren opened his laptop and hit the power button. He entered a search for "missing teen + Cider Creek" and then sat back. "There are a few hits for missing teens but Cider Creek is crossed out."

"What if we try 'missing teen plus Texas'?" she asked.

The results narrowed by a slim margin.

"We can scan the headlines to see if we recognize any of the towns nearby," he said.

"Here's one that isn't far," Darren said. Robb City was forty-five minutes east. "The missing person is a high-school sophomore. Tandra St. Claire is her name."

"Any details about the case?" she asked, scooting closer to him so she could read the print on the screen.

"She's been gone almost two weeks now," he said.

"What about the family?" she asked. "Did they make a statement?"

"The father swears his little girl was taken and that she didn't run away," he said. "Mother blames the father for cheating on her and asking for a divorce."

"Trouble at home," Reese said quietly. It sounded a little too familiar.

"They might speak to us if we can find their address," he said.

"I happen to know Camree Lynn's mom still lives at the same place," Reese said. "We could go talk to her. A lot of time has passed, and she might have done her own searching for her daughter. She could have information that could help us tie the cases together."

"Let's go," he said, checking the time as he bit back a yawn. It was eight o'clock.

Reese glanced down at her clothing, or lack thereof. "I can't go out like this."

"I probably have something in the laundry room for you to borrow," he said.

She shot him a look that said she didn't want to wear another woman's clothes, especially if it was someone he was dating, had dated or had been married to.

"Stacie left a jogging suit here once," he explained. "You two look to be about the same size."

She wanted to ask why Stacie was leaving clothing at his home but suspected it was a sure sign someone was staking a claim. As if the way the doctor had treated Reese earlier wasn't enough to convey the message. Since her only other option was a T-shirt and bathrobe, she agreed. Liking the idea wasn't a requirement. Going outside half-naked was probably still frowned on.

Facing Camree Lynn's mother wasn't something she was looking forward to. Virginia must have been devastated. After losing her only daughter, Virginia didn't show up to school anymore. To be honest, the whole time period was fuzzy for Reese. When Stacie mentioned the part about the brain blocking out trauma for survival purposes, it had resonated. Reese was sure she'd done that exact thing to avoid thinking of her best friend's disappearance.

As much as Darren seemed overprotective of his daughters now, she'd read kids were at far greater risk of being abducted by a stranger at around age fifteen, like Camree Lynn. It was an early stage of independence, a phase of rebelling against parents and testing boundaries. Camree Lynn had fallen into the right age category, but Reese doubted that her friend would do something foolish like meet in person with someone she didn't know from the internet. Besides, the law would have checked her computer and social media sites. At least, Reese hoped that would be the case. The past sheriff had been a little too quick to classify Camree Lynn as a runaway. Was there something in her journal that Reese didn't know about? As close as they'd been, it wasn't impossible to think her friend had kept some secrets to herself.

Teenage years were hard enough with hormones and all the insecurities that came with transitioning from a fully dependent kid to an independent adult. There wasn't enough money in the world to make Reese want to go back to those days. The only bright spot in high school after Camree Lynn's disappearance had been Darren, and she'd broken his heart. He was right about one thing. The toughest years for his girls were ahead. Stacie seemed plenty eager to step into the role of mother.

There must be a story behind the way she looked at him. One that ran deeper than her loving the girls and wanting to pitch in to help because she missed her sister. Those two things might be true, but Reese had picked up on more.

Darren returned with the offering, folded up in outstretched arms. Reese took the warm-ups. Now, she was going to get to wear the woman's clothing. That wouldn't go over too well if they ran into Stacie. Reese hoped it wouldn't happen. She had a feeling

Stacie believed Reese was homing in on what she'd designated as her turf.

Reese had a few choice words for Stacie should the woman confront her. Besides, she'd known Darren first.

Clearly, she was going down a rabbit hole. "I'll be right back."

Five minutes later, she was changed and ready to go. The jogging suit fit well enough. A little tight in the chest area, but she could make it work. Besides, beggars couldn't be choosers, as the saying went.

Could she get information from Virginia Bowles? Or would her former best friend's mother slam the door in Reese's face?

DARREN DIDN'T HAVE shoes that would fit Reese and she couldn't go out barefoot. So when she came out of the bathroom wearing her shoes, he was relieved.

"I cleaned them," she said, motioning toward her ballet flats. "Kept them because I didn't figure they would be much use as evidence, and I needed something to use to walk." She issued a sharp breath and her face twisted up like she was in pain. "Ballet flats and sweatpants—high fashion at its best."

Darren couldn't help but chuckle. He'd read on the society page about her career. Small-town Girl Breaks into Dallas Fashion Scene.

"Let's roll," he said, leading the way to his vehicle.

It was a quarter after nine by the time they made it to the home of Virginia Bowles. Lights were still on.

"Do you know if Mrs. Bowles ever remarried?"

Reese asked Darren as they sat in his idling vehicle in front of her house in the cul-de-sac with half-acre lots.

"I heard she did," he said. "Couldn't say how it worked out, though."

"Guess we'll find out," Reese said. "I just wasn't sure if I should still call her Mrs. Bowles."

On the ride over, Reese had closed her eyes and leaned her head against the headrest. The quiet didn't bother him. It was a rare moment in a house, or car ride, for that matter, when there was peace. Being around Reese reminded him of feelings that had been dormant too long. Delving into the past also reminded him how dangerous secrets were. He'd held on to his for a long time. Could he use Reese as a sounding board? Test the waters by telling her the one he'd been holding in?

The quiet gave him time to think rather than just blow and go 24/7. Thankfully, he worked outside fixing fences and caring for his family's ranch, which was small in comparison to Hayes Cattle. At this point, it was a legacy to his girls should they want it, and taking over kept him close to the land he loved, unlike Reese who couldn't get out of town fast enough.

Was she happy?

Had her life in Dallas worked out the way she'd hoped? Or maybe it was as simple as needing to get far away from Cider Creek and…him.

He'd nursed a bruised ego over that one for longer than he cared to admit.

"I'm sure she'll recognize you," he said. "Let her

lead the way on the conversation and we should be fine."

"Okay," Reese agreed, rubbing her temples as though staving off a severe headache. The ibuprofen was back at the house. He regretted not grabbing the bottle. They could stop on the way home if they could find an open store. Cider Creek and the surrounding area practically rolled up the streets by eight o'clock at night. To eat out later, he would have to go to Austin.

"Are you?" he asked. "Okay?"

"My head feels like it's splitting in two," she said. "Other than that, I'm peachy."

Her attempt to lighten the mood made him crack a smile. Not because the joke was good. In fact, it was corny. It was the way she made eyes at him, like they suddenly went back in time and she made that same goofy expression she used to whenever she tried to make him laugh.

They had laughed, which was something he didn't do a whole lot of anymore, not even with his girls. At least, not like this. The ranch barely made ends meet and he was determined to keep everything running without hiring anyone. If he sold his place, it would cut down on expenses but there was something unsettling about taking over the home his parents had built their life in despite buying fold-up cribs for the place. Too painful?

"What is it?" Reese asked. He glanced over and realized she was studying him.

"Family stuff," he said, dismissing the conversation with his tone.

"I'm here if you want to talk," she said. "Which, I mean, you probably don't want to after all the bad blood between us. It's okay. I mean, I understand why you wouldn't want to talk to me, of all people, about your family."

She always repeated words when she was nervous and was having a hard time spitting out what she wanted to stay.

"I'll keep that in mind," he said, unable to throw her a bone. Her time in town was temporary and his life was too busy for casual friendships with people who lived far away. Besides, why should he trust her again? "Ready?"

Darren cut off the engine to his SUV.

"As much as I'll ever be," she said after a pause.

He got out of the vehicle and then rounded the front. It might have been a long time since he'd had a female over the age of two inside his SUV, but he hadn't forgotten the manners ingrained in him. He opened the passenger door and held out a hand to help her down. She took the offering and the electricity he'd been doing his best to avoid crackled in the air between them, vibrating up his arm, his elbow and into his chest.

Darren sighed. She was still as beautiful, if not more. From the dark-roast hair to eyes so beautiful they looked right through him, Reese Hayes made heads turn, including his. This close, it was hard to breathe. It was almost like his ribs were locked in a vise.

Since staring into her eyes was a mistake, he turned toward the ranch-style brick home. Reese took the hint and led the way. There was no gate or fence in the front yard. None visible on the side, either.

They were able to walk right up to the front door and knock. A little yippee-sounding bark, if it could be called that, fired off from the other side. It only took a few seconds for the porch light to flip on.

Reese positioned herself in front of the peephole. Mrs. Bowles, or whatever her last name was now, would hopefully recognize Reese and open the door. Folks might be friendly but they were known to have a shotgun around, too, so Darren made sure he kept his hands where someone on the other side of the door could see them.

"Mrs. Bowles?" Reese asked. "It's me. Reese Hayes."

Darren didn't want to get too caught up in the fact Reese wasn't married. One thing was certain— he wanted to throw a punch if he ever saw his uncle again. Matias never showed his face again after luring Reese away from town with a paid summer internship in Dallas. The man was considerably older than Reese, seventeen years to be exact. And though, technically she'd been an adult—she'd turned eighteen on April twentieth—a thirty-five-year-old had a helluva lot more experience under his belt.

Even so, it had been a little too easy for her to cast Darren aside. Some of those wounds must still be tender if he was thinking about it while standing on the porch of the mother of a friend who'd been missing for thirteen years.

## Chapter Nine

The door opened a crack and someone picked up the barking beast. A sliver of Camree Lynn's mother's face could be seen. From the looks of her, the last thirteen years had been hard.

"Reese?" Virginia Bowles, or whatever her last name was now, sounded like she was in shock.

"Yes, ma'am," Reese responded. "It's me. And I know it's been a long time but—"

The door swung open and in the next second Reese was being brought into a hug. "I didn't think I'd ever see you again. Heard you'd moved to Dallas and dusted this town off your boots years ago." Virginia took a step back. "Let me look at you." Tears welled in the older woman's eyes. This might have been what Camree Lynn would have looked like if she'd lived into her midfifties. Platinum-blond hair, brown eyes and a heart-shaped face. Mrs. Bowles's skin had that worn-in, leathery look. Too much time in the sun during Texas summers could easily add years to a face. She had sunspots and a mole just above her lip, just like the one Camree Lynn had.

Reese fought back the sudden urge to cry. "May we come in?"

Mrs. Bowles stood there, stunned. She shook her head like she was shaking off a brain fog. "Of course."

The door swung open, and it seemed Mrs. Bowles noticed Darren for the first time. "You're the Pierce boy."

"Darren. Yes, ma'am," he said, his voice smooth as silk. He had a deep timbre now that had a way of sliding over Reese and through her. He seemed able to touch a place deep inside her that no one had discovered.

"Come in," the older woman said, holding her arm out. She was dressed in work clothes despite the late hour. "I'm catching up on emails. Don't mind the mess."

She walked them into the eat-in kitchen, which had a laptop and a stack of books. "I'm going back to school, so ignore these and have a seat anywhere you like."

Mrs. Bowles's home had always been spick-and-span, with a place for everything. Only a couple of necessities were allowed to be on the kitchen counters. This place wouldn't exactly qualify for an episode of *Hoarders*, but it would if they had a tidy edition.

"What are you studying?" Reese asked as she took a spot at the table.

"Accounting," she said without hesitation before turning in front of a cabinet. "Can I get either of you something to drink?"

"Water, if it's not too much trouble," Reese said.

Darren nodded. "Same for me."

"Two waters coming right up," she said, smiling. After filling two glasses with ice and water from the fridge, she brought them over and set them down on the table. "It sure is good to see you."

The look in her eyes said it was also painful. No doubt being around Reese brought back a lot of memories of Camree Lynn. She had worried that showing up here would bring back painful memories for the woman.

"What makes you want to study accounting?" Reese asked, unable to find the right words to ask what she really wanted to know, without some type of lead-in.

"Ever since Evan left…" She flashed her eyes at them. "He was my second husband."

Reese nodded.

Camree's mother sighed sharply. "Well, ever since he took off with his bookkeeper, I've had all kinds of time on my hands. Figured I'd find out what was so great about a numbers person."

"I'm sorry to hear it, Mrs.—"

"Virginia," she interrupted. "Please. Call me Virginia."

It would take some getting used to, but Reese figured she could manage. "Will do, Virginia."

The older woman smiled as she took a seat across the table from Reese and Darren. "What can I help you with? I know you didn't come all the way down here from Dallas to find out what I'm studying these days."

"Thank you for seeing us without any advanced warning," Reese began, taking advantage of the opening while hoping the words would flow. "It's about Camree Lynn."

Virginia heaved a sigh, and it looked like her body deflated. "I thought maybe that's the reason you were here." She lifted her gaze and inhaled a breath. "I read about the girl in the news. Tandra. My phone rings every time a reporter digs around in a case that might look anything like my girl."

Reese didn't know one way or the other if the story brought her back near Cider Creek to investigate. Although, it would make sense as the reason she'd gotten herself in danger if she'd been poking around in the wrong place. She cursed trauma for stealing her recent memories.

"Yes," she said, unsure if it was true or not. To be fair, they had just read about Tandra.

"Do you see similarities?" Virginia continued.

"I'm not sure," Reese admitted. "But I'd like to learn more about what happened with Camree Lynn." She put up her hand to stop Virginia from saying anything just yet. "And I know it was a long time ago."

"Dear child," Virginia said. "Where do I even begin? I miss my daughter every day. I wonder if she's alive. I think about what she might have become. Would she have gone to Dallas with you to work, in art and fashion like the two of you always planned? Would she be as successful as you?"

"I'm not—"

"Don't be modest, sweetheart," Virginia protested. "I've followed your career." Her chest puffed out a little. "I've been proud of you."

Tears welled in Reese's eyes. "It means a lot to hear you say that, Virginia."

"You deserve it, dear," Virginia continued. "And I can't help but think the two of you would have stayed lifelong friends."

"That was the plan," Reese stated.

Virginia dropped her gaze. "The divorce was hard on my daughter."

"Yes," Reese agreed. There was no use lying at this point.

"I didn't know what to think at first," Virginia said. "When Camree Lynn first…disappeared. We'd been fighting. The family was a mess." She looked up and searched Reese's eyes. "We never should have dragged her into our marital problems."

"I doubt you could have hidden anything from her," Reese said.

Virginia nodded. "That very well might be true. Still, I believed the law when they said she'd run away."

"And now?"

"No one stays mad this many years, do they," Virginia stated it like it was biblical truth. "She would have come home a few months later, after she'd had a chance to cool off. I tried to tell the sheriff the same thing, but he brushed me off. With the divorce, well, it was a little too easy to say she ran off to Houston or Dallas in an election year. Otherwise, he would have allowed a killer to stalk a young person in his county, right under his nose."

"Doesn't bode well on election day, does it," Darren said. The disdain in his voice reminded her that he'd been friends with Camree Lynn, too.

DARREN CLENCHED HIS back teeth. Being lazy on a job was one thing. A law-enforcement officer being lazy on the job was enough to make him see red. If the sheriff had treated Camree Lynn's case correctly, would she be sitting here at this table with them? Would her mother's smile reach her eyes? Because it sure as hell didn't now, and he couldn't blame Virginia one bit. The thought of losing one of his girls…

His grip around his glass was tight enough to break it, so he forced himself to cool off and set down the glass.

"No. It doesn't," Virginia said about his election-day comment. She placed her palms on the table. "Not a day goes by that I don't think about my Camree Lynn. I called police in Houston, Dallas, Austin. They weren't any help."

Darren could only imagine the pain. He prayed like hell that he would never have to experience something as awful as losing a child.

"Funny thing is, you lose everything with your child," Virginia continued. "Oh, at first everyone is wonderful. They see you at the grocery store and can't wait to give you a hug and tell you what your child meant to them. After a while, it calms down and then you become this visual reminder of how awful it is to lose your baby. Folks see you in the soup aisle and skip it." She waved her hands in the air. "I'm sure they don't mean to come across as coldhearted. It's like they can't face you any longer because you remind them of what *they* could lose."

"I'm so sorry," Reese said with the kind of emotion that said she meant it.

"You were just a child yourself," Virginia said. "I imagine you were doing the best you could just to survive every day."

"For the record, I never believed she ran away," Reese stated.

Virginia rocked her head. "I know. Looking back, I should have listened." She studied a spot on the table in front of her. "What's the saying? Something about 'out of the mouths of babes.'"

Reese nodded. Darren had heard the saying, too.

"You're right, though," Reese said. "None of the other adults listened to me, either. Not the sheriff or my grandfather."

Virginia reached across the table for Reese's hands. "He was so hard on you."

"Yes," Reese said. "My mother tried to stick up for me but she was too… I don't know what the right word is."

"Political?" Virginia said.

"A pushover," Reese corrected. "At least in my view."

"Your mother was in a difficult position with your grandfather with the way he held the ranch over her head," Virginia stated, like it was common knowledge.

"What do you mean?" Reese asked.

"He used the ranch to keep her under his thumb," Virginia said. "Don't count your mother out, though.

She was as strong as they come but she'd never worked a day in her life outside of the family business. Duncan used it against her, too. The bastard."

Reese's surprise was written all over her face. "Hold on a minute. Are you telling me that my mother would have happily left the ranch if my grandfather hadn't threatened her with the purse strings?"

"That's right," Virginia confirmed. "He must have realized she would leave after her husband..." Virginia locked gazes with Reese for a few seconds. "Logan died. Your mother had six hungry mouths to feed. Seven if you count your grandmother, who was from a generation of women who didn't have the option of making their own living. She had medical bills, too. Your grandfather on your father's side threatened to cut your mother off if she didn't bring you all up on the ranch."

Reese sucked in a breath. "I'm starting to understand my mother a little better."

"Marla was a strong woman," Virginia said. "I've always admired her for doing what was right for her family even when it put her in a bad position. She knew how to be delicate, whereas I was always more headstrong in life."

"The two of you were friends?" Reese asked, surprised.

"As much as we could be considering our lives were so different," Virginia said. "Our daughters, however, were best friends and we both approved. I'm afraid I was so caught up in my own misery with my first husband that I neglected Camree Lynn. And then she was gone. For months, I believed she hated me. That she couldn't wait to leave home to get away from the fights. I can't count the number of times she threatened to run off." Virginia covered her mouth with her hand, like the words were almost too horrible to speak out loud. A few tears rolled down her cheeks. "I'm sorry." She shook her head. "You would think it would get easier. It's just, I never really talk about her anymore. Her father and I lost contact after the divorce. Without her, there wasn't much left for us to talk about. And then my second husband didn't know her, so I just stopped."

"I have twin baby girls," Darren stated. "Every day, I make mistakes with them. I worry if my tone of voice is too harsh or if they're sleeping all right. I check their cribs several times a night to make sure they're still breathing."

Virginia smiled through tears that ran freely down her face. "How old?"

"Eighteen months," he responded.

"How precious," Virginia said. "Do you have pictures?"

He fished his cell phone out of his pocket and thumbed through the pass code before tapping the photo icon. A smile crept across his mouth as the first photo filled the screen. "Here they are in all their glory." He turned the screen so Virginia could see.

"They're beautiful," she said as her gaze immediately shifted to study him and Reese. "I can't tell which one of you they favor the most."

"Oh, they're not mine," Reese said. "I'm not… haven't been… We haven't seen each other in years."

Virginia balked. "I wondered how you would have pulled off a secret wedding and a life working in two different cities."

"That would be impossible," Reese said with a little too much enthusiasm. He tried not to be offended that she seemed so ready to ship him off with someone else. Anyone else. He resisted the urge to say the logistics might be tricky but not impossible. Not for two people who were in love. With technology, long distance was no longer an issue. Except he could admit that he needed someone in the same area now that the twins were in his life.

Virginia looked like she was biting her tongue. Yes, they'd been a couple in high school, but she must not be aware of the fact Reese had easily chucked their relationship for a job then dated his uncle, no less.

"We went our separate ways after high school," he said, figuring it summed up the past in the most respectful way to both of them. "We had different goals." He also didn't see the need to point out her goal had been to date the first man who came along with a job offer. That was probably being harsh and he was most likely speaking from his ego—an ego that had taken more than its fair share of hits years ago.

Hazel might not have lit the same fires inside him as Reese, but he'd loved his wife in his own way. A voice in the back of his head reminded him that she'd betrayed him, too. Maybe that was just his curse with the opposite sex. They were bound to deceive him at some point.

"Did the law ever return any of Camree's personal belongings?" Reese asked after clearing her throat. The change in subject was a welcomed reprieve.

Virginia handed his phone back to him. "Yes. As a matter of fact, they did. Said nothing was relevant to a runaway case."

"What about her journal?" Reese continued.

"Still under her mattress," Virginia said. "I put it there because I knew she'd be so angry if she knew we'd read it."

Reese shifted in her seat. "Mind if I take a look?"

# Chapter Ten

Virginia studied Reese as though the woman was trying to make up her mind as to just how bad of an idea it might be to disturb Camree Lynn's things again.

"Please," Reese added for good measure.

"What would be the point?" Virginia asked. "Unless you think you can bring her back by rooting through her things." Virginia blew out a breath. "I always felt guilty for letting the sheriff read her personal thoughts. Then again, I thought she'd come back once she cooled off."

Reese feared Camree Lynn was gone forever. A body had never been found. There was no closure for anyone who missed her. For a split second, she saw an image of Virginia sitting at this table, staring at that front door, expecting her daughter to come busting through in a fit of rage about her journal becoming public property. It made her sad all over again. The kind of sadness that had her cry in her pillow every night and refuse to go to school or speak to anyone other than the law or Darren. Sheriff Webb had been the sheriff back then. He'd had asked a few questions about Camree Lynn's mental state but even then, Reese believed the man had made up his mind. Looking back, talking to her had been ticking a box on a form rather than digging for information in an investigation. To Sheriff Webb, it had been an open-and-shut case.

"I'd like to explore any similarities, like we said before," Reese said honestly.

"It won't bring her back," Virginia protested.

"No. I'm sorry, but it won't. It might bring closure and justice, though," Reese pointed out.

"Camree Lynn isn't here to tell me what she wants one way or the other." Virginia threw her hands up in the air. "So I guess it won't do any harm now."

"We can see the journal then?" Reese asked, just to be certain they were on the same page. Getting a close-up look at how hard parenting was made her soften toward her own mother. Seeing Darren second-guess himself as a dad brought home how difficult the job must be. Hearing about the ultimatum her mother had faced burned her up even more about her no-good grandfather. What had the man done for the family besides build a successful cattle ranch? Reese had walked away from the family money at eighteen and had no plans to ask for a red cent. The money wasn't hers. She hadn't worked for it and had no business taking it as far as she was concerned.

Virginia stood up and placed her palms on the table as she leaned toward them. "Yes. You can see the journal. I've read over it a dozen times and couldn't find any clues. But you knew her better than anyone else." She shrugged. "Maybe you'll find something the rest of us missed. By the time we realized she wasn't coming back, the trail was cold."

"I'll do my best," Reese promised.

Virginia excused herself and went down the hallway. Darren had been quiet during the journal discussion. He sat back with his arms folded. Had Reese said something to offend him? His jaw muscle ticked like he was clenching his back teeth. It could be the heaviness of the situation, the fact that his daughters lived in a small town where a crime this heinous could occur or he was angry with her. She'd seen the look before. Usually, it meant the latter.

"Everything okay?" she asked, figuring it was better to speak up now than hold her tongue.

"Sure," he responded with a tone that said the opposite was true.

Reese wasn't ready to let it go. "Did I say something wrong?"

Before he could respond, Virginia came back into the room, holding Camree Lynn's journal high in the air. *The Starry Night* had been Camree Lynn's favorite painting. She'd been obsessed with it, so her journal was wrapped in a cover with a picture of the famous oil painting. "Here it is."

"Do you mind if we take it with us?" Reese asked.

Virginia emphatically shook her head. "In a strange way, I feel like she might come home expecting it to be tucked underneath her mattress. If it goes…"

Overwrought with emotion, the older woman struggled to get the words out. Reese could only imagine how difficult it must be for Virginia to sit across the table from her presumably dead daughter's former best friend.

She handed over the journal. "Take pictures of anything you want, but the journal must stay here."

"Okay," Reese said, taking the offering as Virginia reclaimed her seat across the table from them. Reese couldn't help but reach out for Virginia's hand to comfort her. She had no idea if the gesture made a difference, but when Virginia looked at her with gratitude in her eyes, Reese was humbled.

There'd been the occasional interaction with Virginia in a grocery-store parking lot years ago. Or a wave at the post office. But this was different. They were speaking to each other as adults who were on the same page about what had happened to Virginia's daughter and Reese's best friend.

Reese was also seeing parenting in a new light, and the job was even harder than she'd imagined it would be. Had she been too hard on her own mother? Judged her too harshly when Reese didn't have all the facts? The hard answer was yes. But she wished her mother had mentioned the ultimatum or explained the reasons she stuck around when Duncan Hayes had been a class-A jerk.

She liked her grandfather even less now and she didn't think that was even possible.

Refocusing on the journal, she flipped page after page until she reached the end. There were mostly scribbles, random thoughts, and sketches. She'd forgotten how much Camree Lynn liked to draw.

"She was good, wasn't she?" Virginia asked as Reese used her index finger to trace the outline of a teddy-bear drawing on the last page.

"Very," Reese agreed.

"She was going to start taking art classes in Austin on Saturdays," Virginia said.

"I didn't know that," Reese replied.

"Because I hadn't told her yet," Virginia said wistfully. "Her father and I decided to find classes for her as a way of apologizing for all the arguing we did with her around." She flashed her eyes at Reese and then Darren. "If you do nothing else as a parent, hold your temper. Count to ten. Walk out of the room. And I don't just mean with your children. Do it with your spouse as well."

"Thank you for the advice," he said with genuine appreciation in his tone. "My wife died a year ago."

Reese's heart nearly cracked in half at hearing him talk about the mother of his children to Virginia.

"I'm on this road by myself," he said. "It's nice to get a female perspective, and from someone who has a lot of experience."

Virginia clutched the center of her chest. "Dear boy. I remember you being a handful in your youth." She looked at him with such appreciation. "Look how you've grown into an amazing person. Your girls are lucky to have you. And don't you think for a second you're not going to be enough."

Darren nodded. "Thank you."

Virginia sucked in a breath. "I just remembered something. The sheriff never took me seriously because I believed my daughter ran away for a long time, but then I remembered two people had interactions with her that, looking back, made me think twice."

"Who were they?" Reese asked, leaning into her elbows that were already on the edge of the table.

"Phillip Rhodes and…" She snapped her fingers but Reese's body tensed at the mention of that name.

DARREN WITNESSED A change in Reese. It was almost as though her muscles coiled. He made a mental note to ask her about it in the SUV on the way back because her lips pressed together like they were locked.

"And the Archer boy," Virginia continued. "What was his first name?"

"They have three boys in that family. All close in age," Darren said as Reese seemed to have suddenly gone mute. "Andrew, Alexander or Aiden?"

"Aiden," Virginia confirmed. "Aiden Archer."

"What made you suspicious of these two?" Darren asked.

"Phillip Rhodes was a summer camp counselor at the Camp Needles," Virginia said. "He seemed to take an extra interest in Camree Lynn when he was here, but he always got nervous if he saw me."

Darren didn't put a lot of stock into the comment. "That could be any teenager around a girl's mom, especially one he likes."

Virginia nodded. "That's true, but I would see him stand close to her with his back turned to me. Later, I found out he wasn't a teenager even though he looked like one. He was twenty-four at the time of her disappearance."

"Did the law list him as someone she might have run off with?" Darren asked.

"I'm not sure if you remember but the camp closed the next year, so he never came back. The sheriff dismissed my concern. Said there was no evidence linking Rhodes to Camree Lynn because no crime had been committed."

"She was fifteen at the time she went missing," Darren said.

Virginia's lips thinned. "The sheriff said fifteen was the most common age for runaways. He said she'd be back once she realized how hard life was. Said she'd most likely return home on her own accord by month's end."

Darren took in a deep breath to calm his rising anger. It was impossible not to imagine this happening to one of his daughters and the lengths to which he would have gone to locate her and bring her home. No judgment on Virginia, but he wouldn't have been able to sleep until his daughters were tucked into their own beds again.

"When she didn't come back, did he have an excuse?" Darren asked.

"He'd already tried to track her cell phone," she said. "Couldn't find anything out of the ordinary on the call logs that ended the day before she left."

The lawman had mishandled the case from day one. He'd read somewhere that the first twenty-four hours were the most critical in an investigation. After twenty-four hours, trails went cold. Probably less than that when it came to children and stranger abductions.

"The person who abducted her could have made sure there would have been no way to track them," he countered, realizing he was preaching to the choir when Virginia nodded.

There was something to be said for a mother's intuition. He made a mental note of the two names Virginia had supplied. The first one would be difficult to track and he had no idea what Aiden was up to now. Darren didn't keep up with folks in his own grade, let alone kids who were two years older.

Virginia bit back a yawn. Her red-rimmed eyes looked like they were trying to close on her. Dredging up the past had to be awful for her. His heart went out to Camree's mother.

"Is there anything else you remember about that time?" he asked, figuring they'd learned enough for one evening. Besides, he wanted to get Reese home and to bed. She'd been through more than anyone should have to endure and needed sleep.

"Just those two names stick out in my mind," she said on a shrug. "As far as the other one goes, Aiden Archer, I didn't like the way he was always watching her when he was around. I asked if he ever tried to speak to her and she said he gave her the creeps. She brushed him off." She stopped and took in a deep breath. "What I wouldn't give to go back and do things differently with Camree Lynn. Hug her more. Tell her how much I love her." More tears streamed down Virginia's cheeks. She apologized as she wiped them away. "I certainly would have gone back and talked to those men once I suspected she didn't run away."

"No need to be sorry," he said to her as he stood up.

"I was drinking a lot back then to cope with the end of my marriage," Virginia admitted with an embarrassed look.

Reese closed the journal and scooted it across the table toward Virginia, who took it and then held it against her chest.

"Thank you for talking to us tonight," Reese finally said but it sounded like there was a frog in her throat. "It's really good to see you again."

"Stop by anytime," Virginia said, meeting them around the table. With her free arm, she embraced Reese in a quick hug. "She would be proud of you. You know that, right? You're doing everything the two of you said you would. You're successful in Dallas, organizing runway shows for designers. She was into art. You're successful and Camree Lynn is bursting with pride somewhere."

"It means a lot to hear you say that," Reese said. The hitch in her throat said she was holding back. It probably shouldn't surprise him that Reese had secrets. She'd kept a big one from him right up until she took off.

"I mean every word," Virginia said as she walked them to the door. She put her hand on Darren's shoulder. "If you ever want to talk…give me a call or come on by. I'd love to meet your girls someday."

"Will do, ma'am," he said.

Reese was quiet on the way to the SUV. He walked

her to the passenger side with his hand on her elbow. Getting close to her was probably a bad idea on his part, but he could tell being in Camree Lynn's house again, seeing her journal, had nearly knocked Reese on her backside.

After opening the door and offering a hand, he helped her with the big step up to the passenger seat. One look at her said the adrenaline rush she'd been running on had expired. He rounded the front of the SUV, and then reclaimed the driver's seat.

It only took a few seconds to buckle up. He glanced over and noticed Reese wasn't wearing hers.

"You might want to put your seat belt on or this thing will start griping at you," he said, motioning toward the screen in his dash. Everything had technology in it now.

Reese stared ahead with a blank look on her face. "I recognized one of those names."

## Chapter Eleven

"Phillip Rhodes." Reese involuntarily shivered after saying the name out loud. She buckled up so Darren could get on the road.

"The camp counselor?" Darren asked.

She nodded.

"He gave me the creeps. I even warned Camree Lynn about him. She seemed on the same page about avoiding the guy after he showed up in the barn and came on to me," she explained.

"Why was he there in the first place?" he asked.

"Duncan hired him for seasonal work after the camp closed for the summer," she said. "I'd forgotten all about him and the incident until Virginia brought him up again just now. I just wanted to block it out after it happened."

"Did you tell the sheriff about him before?" Darren asked.

Reese shook her head. "There didn't seem to be a reason to at the time. I mean, Camree Lynn didn't want to be around him to my knowledge. I feel like she would have told me if that changed at some point."

"Teenagers can be secretive," he said.

She nodded. No one in the community knew what a jerk her grandfather was to his family. All of the Hayes kids had been trained to keep the secret even though Reese didn't recall a particular conversation. It was ingrained in them not to discuss family matters outside of Hayes Ranch. Ranch hands were required to sign NDAs, so they legally couldn't discuss anything that went on.

"What exactly did Phillip Rhodes do to you?" Darren asked as he white-knuckled the steering wheel.

The memory was so traumatic, she'd blocked it out. The details were coming back now, though, and they made her hands fist. "He cornered me in a stall, pushed me up against the wall and tried to force me to kiss him."

"But you fought back," he said.

"Hell, yes, I did," she said. "He had grabby hands that were ridiculously strong. He pinned mine above my head easily." She needed a second to breathe through the tightening in her chest at the horrific memory that she'd suppressed for so long. "I wasn't going down willingly, so he dropped a hand and forced my face to be still." Bile burned the back of her throat as she thought about it now. "I was young, so I panicked. I was somehow afraid the whole incident would be twisted around to become my fault. Duncan was so hard on us, especially the girls."

"That son of a bitch," Darren said under his breath. It was so low, she almost didn't hear him. She had no idea if he was talking about Phillip or Duncan, but the label fit both, in her opinion. Phillip for being a jerk and Duncan for making her afraid to speak up.

More of the memory surfaced. "He licked my neck, which was disgusting, and then dropped his hand from my jaw and grabbed..." She didn't need to go into detail. The thought of what he did alone made her cringe. "Thankfully, my brother Tiernan came walking into the barn. Phillip threatened me if I told on him, and I clamped my mouth shut while he pretended to be helping me clean out the stall."

"Tiernan didn't catch on to what was going on?" Darren asked.

"I'm a very good actress," she explained. "So, no. But I suspect he had questions since I was shaken up. Before he could ask, I brushed the whole incident off."

Darren's silence hurt her feelings because he gave a small nod of agreement about her being a good actress. She didn't have a right to be mad at him. She'd kept a secret from him years ago when his uncle had first offered her an internship. She'd had to conceal the information or risk being shut down by her grandfather. And, honestly, talking to Darren face-to-face might have made her change her mind and stay. Dating Darren's uncle had been her worst regret. Matias Ossian had been the opposite of everything she'd known in Cider Creek. He wore hand-tailored suits and shiny shoes. He drove a sports car when she was used to pickup trucks and SUVs. On top of that, he had connections to a world in which she desperately wanted to belong.

The Hayes family had money, so his show of money

wasn't what had impressed her—it was the way he carried himself. He was older, mysterious. In the beginning, though, she had no idea they would end up dating. Being alone in Dallas without family or friends turned out to be harder than she realized it would be. Matias had offered to bring over dinner a few times, so she wouldn't have to eat alone. Slowly but surely, he'd broken down her defenses and preyed on her loneliness. In fact, he'd played her like a fine instrument, all the while betraying her behind her back. She'd done it to herself, too, and was far too proud to admit she'd made a mistake. Tucking her tail between her legs and going home hadn't been an option. Not to someone with a stubborn streak a mile long.

Mistakes were always hard to admit, even harder to face.

He started the engine and put the gearshift into Drive, then pulled onto the farm road leading toward his home. He mumbled something about wishing he could spend five minutes alone in a locked room with the bastard. She assumed he was referring to Phillip, since he couldn't exactly read her thoughts. There'd been a time when she would have sworn he could. But that was a long time ago, he'd been proven wrong and a lot had changed since then.

Missed opportunities were the worst. But then, looking back, if she had stayed and—on the off chance—had actually married Darren, then he wouldn't have his beautiful twins. His life would look very different, and as much as he complained about being tired, his eyes lit up at every mention of those babies. So much so that Reese wanted to meet them to see what the fuss was all about. She'd never been much of a baby person. There were no longings about being pregnant or fantasizing about a wedding. Her brothers seemed to have found true love and she was happy for each and every one of them. Those things were great for other people.

And yet, being around Darren now did have her wondering what life might have been like if she'd made a different choice. But she couldn't have him and Dallas. Leaving Cider Creek had been a necessity and she was proud of herself for the career she'd built so far. She'd needed to know she could not just survive on her own, but make something of her life outside of Hayes Cattle. Surely, Darren could understand.

"Once we get back to my place, I'll do a little digging into Phillip Rhodes's current situation," he finally said. "He's a bastard but that doesn't mean he abducted Camree Lynn or Tandra. To be honest, I think I blanked out most of that time period of life."

"Same for me," she admitted. At least he was talking again. The silence had given her mind too much time to spiral. "A lot of the details are fuzzy." The thought of digging into her friend's disappearance made her stomach tie in knots, but she would face anything at this point for answers.

He nodded as he stared out the front windshield at the stretch of road in front of them.

"For what it's worth, I never had to 'act' when it came to how I felt for you," she said.

"Okay," he responded. The one word combined with his serious expression gave her the impression he would never be able to put the past behind them. She didn't expect him to run toward her with open arms, but a small hope had been building inside her that they could be friends. The wishful thinking was off base. She needed to remind herself of that fact every hour if necessary until it sunk in.

"WHAT ARE YOUR thoughts on Aiden Archer?"

The question from Reese yanked Darren out of his heavy thoughts. Those thoughts had gone on a path of their own the minute she mentioned being a convincing actress. He could personally attest to her abilities, considering he'd been the last to know she was planning to shred his heart and leave town. The breakup text from her had come when she was already halfway to her new city.

"I have no idea what he's up to these days. I never really liked the family, but that doesn't make one of them a criminal," he said.

"True," she responded. "As far as Phillip goes, I'd be interested to see if it's common for someone like him to escalate to something as extreme as kidnapping. I mean, I read somewhere that Peeping Toms actually do progress to break-ins and raping victims."

He nodded and mulled over the information on the rest of the ride home. It was getting late and Reese had had one helluva long day, so she needed rest.

As he pulled up in front of his home, he said, "I'm good without sleep for a few hours. Why don't you grab a nap and then I'll have an update for you."

"What about the girls?" she asked.

It was probably wrong to allow his heart to be warmed by the fact that her first thought was his children. "They'll be fine. I'll swing by at some point in the morning to check on them." He didn't like going more than a day without seeing them for himself, which had been a challenge during calving season without Hazel.

Reese didn't wait for him to come around to the passenger side before she exited the SUV.

She waited at the door for him to unlock it. The move surprised him at first, because he couldn't remember the last time he'd locked a door. With everything going on, he felt the need to now. He thought about increasing security with cameras and possibly an alarm, and hated the thought that his daughters might grow up in a world where they didn't feel free to come and go as they pleased.

Once inside, exhaustion started to hit him, too. He bit back a yawn, figuring he had another hour in him before he'd need to grab a few minutes of shut-eye.

"Mind if I curl up on the couch?" Reese asked as she twisted her fingers together. "The thought of being alone in a room right now..." She shuddered.

"Go ahead and make yourself comfortable while I grab a pillow and a blanket," he said, then exited the room. He returned a minute later to find her standing at the kitchen sink, drinking a glass of water. "Are you hungry?"

"A little bit, but I should probably get some rest," she said. "I'm so tired my legs ache."

He nodded, then made up the couch. It looked comfortable enough, although he couldn't imagine fitting on it with his six-feet-three-inch frame.

"I'll just change back into sleeping clothes," she said. It was her turn to disappear for a few minutes. He shouldn't like seeing her wearing his AC/DC T-shirt as much as he did, but Reese was a beautiful woman and they had a lot of good history before the one big bad event. It had been a heartbreaker, to be sure, but the old saying "don't throw the baby out with the bath-water" was beginning to seem relevant here. This was good. It meant he was starting to get closure. He'd mentioned to Stacie that he might be ready to move on and dip his toe in the dating waters. Shedding the past might allow him to open up to something all the way this time, instead of holding a piece of his heart in reserve for someone who was never coming back.

Reese positioned herself on the couch as he walked into the kitchen to make coffee.

He had no idea what her sleep habits were since they'd practically been kids when they'd dated and a lot could change. "Will noises bother you?"

"Not today they won't," she said. Her sleepy voice tugged at his heartstrings.

"You used to be a heavy sleeper, but I wasn't sure if that stuck," he admitted.

"I've slept through a tornado alarm that was right outside my bedroom window," she said. "So, yeah, some things will never change."

He didn't need to pay too close attention to what did or didn't change when it came to Reese.

She curled up on her side. From this vantage point,

he couldn't see if she'd closed her eyes, but suspected so. After grabbing his laptop, he hit the power button, bringing his screen to life. Time to do a little digging into the cases and see if he could find any similarities.

The first name he typed in was Camree Lynn's. There were a couple of social media accounts with the name but no news stories of her disappearance. Then again, she'd been classified as a runaway. That fact was going to make this harder than he wanted it to be.

They would have to gain information by talking to folks. He could start with Stacie. She'd grown up not far from here. Her parents might know something. But the people who would remember the most were related to Reese. Her mother would have taken a keen interest in the case, considering it was her daughter's best friend. Then there was Granny. She was a firecracker with a great memory. She might have paid special attention to what was going on.

Between him and Reese, maybe they could piece together what happened or get enough to find a similarity with the Tandra disappearance. At least her parents were on the same page.

Based on the photo of Tandra, she and Camree Lynn were similar-looking with dirty blond hair and cobalt-blue eyes. Both were fifteen and Tandra's parents admitted to talking about divorce, which was hard on any kid, but especially a teenager going through an independent streak.

The crimes occurred in neighboring counties. Darren suspected they could be related. He wondered how many other missing teens around the state had the same physical attributes. It was impossible to tell whether or not Tandra was the same height as Camree Lynn, but they had similar builds.

Scanning the search results of "missing or runaway teenage girls" in the news section, he located three other females in between Camree Lynn and Tandra who looked similar to them. All from Texas and spread around the state. He opened a document and made a note of their names and any family information he could find. If the same person was responsible for Camree Lynn and Tandra's disappearances, he'd chosen girls who had tumultuous family lives.

It was tempting to wake up Reese with this find, but he didn't want to disrupt her soft, even breathing.

A possible pattern was emerging, though. And Sheriff Courtright needed to be asked some hard questions.

## Chapter Twelve

Reese opened her eyes, stretched and yawned. Light filtered through the slats of the miniblinds, so it must be morning. A figure was slumped over in a chair in the living room. A shirtless figure. The figure was Darren. Had he slept in that uncomfortable position all night long so she wouldn't be alone?

The least she could do was make coffee and cook breakfast. She freshened up in the bathroom before folding up her blanket and then stacking it on top of the pillow. With care, she sidestepped a squeaky toy and made it into the next room quietly.

The supplies for coffee were easy to find. His kitchen was orderly, so mugs were in the cabinet above the machine.

The living area might be messy with all the kid stuff lying around, but the kitchen had a place for everything. There were no dishes in the sink. He'd come a long way considering his mother used to be on him almost constantly to put his dishes in the dishwasher.

Darren Pierce was a grown-up now. She smiled. Sleep put her in a better mood. It helped that her head didn't feel like it was split in two this morning. Caffeine would clear the cobwebs. Food would keep her from getting queasy.

Once the coffee was working, she checked the fridge. There was a carton of eggs. There were green onions and bell peppers. She snagged shredded cheese and milk. With these ingredients, she could fix a mean omelet.

"What is that smell?" Darren asked. His deep voice raised goose bumps on her arms and caused warmth to spread through her. "Heaven?"

"My version," she said, turning her head enough to see him push to standing. The six-pack in his stomach was more like a twelve-pack. She forced her gaze back on the frying pan. "Almost done."

"What can I do to help?" he asked.

Being independent and taking care of twins wasn't something she could imagine pulling off on her own. It was high time someone took care of him for a change. "Take a seat at the table."

"You sure?"

The fact that there was a twinge of guilt in his voice, like he believed he should be helping, indicated that this man rarely got a break.

"Positive," she reassured him as she plated the food. She poured a cup of coffee for him and brought both to the table while he rubbed his eyes and yawned. "Eat. Drink. Once you get some caffeine inside you, I'd like to hear about what you found last night in your search."

Reese set down breakfast in front of Darren, who

looked impressed by her cooking skills. A sense of accomplishment brought a smile to her lips. She had no doubt this day was going to be heavy once it got going, so it was nice to have a few quiet minutes this morning to share a meal.

After making her own breakfast, she joined him.

"When did you learn to cook?" he asked with a grin.

"Cooking shows." She returned the smile. "I know. Go figure. But you can learn just about anything you want to on the internet when you can't sleep at three o'clock in the morning."

"I'm surprised you have any time after hearing about your dedication to your job last night," he said.

"A girl has to eat," she said explained. "My mom was a good cook and takeout gets old." She shrugged. "I found a couple of shows that I liked and, more importantly, could pause as I followed along. Turns out, cooking isn't as awful or hard as I thought it would be. And I have a lot of satisfaction in knowing I can take care of myself."

"So-o-o-o-o." He drew out the word. "Just the omelets then."

"How did you know?" she asked.

"You overexplained your answer. It's always a sign someone is lying," he teased.

"Good to know," she replied. "I'll make sure to give short answers the next time I lie." Reese laughed and so did Darren. It felt good to laugh again. There hadn't been much laughter in her life since she left Cider Creek, and him. He'd always had a way of pulling a smile out of her. Good to know some things didn't change.

The plates were empty too soon, as were the cups. They needed to talk.

"Did you find anything last night in your research?" she asked.

He brought her up to speed.

"That makes five victims that we know about if they're all linked," she said.

"And gives us a trail to work with," he said. "We have two names to start with and we can track them down to figure out if they have jobs that travel, for instance."

It sounded like a good place to start. "If we can figure out where they work, we might be able to get a hold of their vacation schedule." Hearing the words made her think differently. "Actually, I think this guy knows his targets. He would have to have a job that put him in those places long enough to find his target. The fact all the parents were in the middle of fighting and facing divorce means he had some kind of inside knowledge into their personal lives."

"Which could mean he contacted them on their computers, or via an app," he deduced as he tapped his finger on the table.

"Wouldn't that leave a cyber trial?" she asked.

"Yes, but these kids are classified as runaways, so no one is investigating too deeply. There are probably programs that can hide online activity," he informed her. "The crimes are occurring around Texas, so no link has been made up until now and we're just guessing here."

She nodded. "True enough. We are just going on flimsy information. We don't have evidence and, based on what you read, no bodies have ever been recovered."

"I imagine it's difficult to prove a murder case without a dead body."

Reese sighed. "This guy moves around to different locations. It's possibly Phillip Rhodes or Aiden Archer. Could be someone else, though."

"I take an accusation like this one very seriously," he said. "No one deserves to have their privacy invaded without clear evidence against them and we can't even prove any of these disappearances are linked."

She didn't want to be pessimistic about their amateur investigation, but they needed to be honest and face facts. "The cases are cold, too." And they might be grasping at straws.

Darren studied the rim of his coffee cup for a long moment before lifting his gaze to meet hers. "All we're doing is asking questions."

She nodded.

"I thought we might want to start with my in-laws and then move to your family," he explained. "We have the best chance of someone remembering or having suspicions if we talk to the people who were closest to Camree Lynn's disappearance. Your family would have followed the story. Your mother, knowing how she is, probably brought meals to Camree Lynn's mother. At the very least, she would have dropped something off at her doorstep."

Why was it so easy to forget the good qualities in

family members and focus on the bad stuff that happened? Reese was beginning to realize how shortsighted she'd been with her mother. In fact, she was starting to feel like a brat for punishing the woman for the behavior of Duncan Hayes. Rather than ask about the circumstances, Reese had made judgments about her mother being too weak to take on Duncan.

It might even be true. But her weak spot had been needing to provide for her children. Food and a roof over their heads cost money—money Duncan had but used to keep his daughter-in-law under his thumb after her husband, who was his son, had died. So, no, she wouldn't mourn a man who could be such a bastard to everyone around him.

But she didn't get off scot-free, either. The day she became independent was the moment she became responsible for her actions. She owed her mother an apology and a conversation.

Calling her couldn't be put off any longer.

DARREN MOVED INTO the bedroom to make the call he needed.

"How are my girls?" he asked the minute his former mother-in-law picked up.

"Amazing," she said, but she sounded more tired than she probably wanted to let on. "They've eaten breakfast and both are in their jumpy things." He could hear giggles in the background and the sound made the world right itself. "Have you had a chance to finish filling out the medical history on your side of the family? The nurse called and said your part has been left blank and they just caught it after the eighteen-month checkup."

"No. I haven't," he said, hating that he kept skirting this issue. The truth was that he wasn't one-hundred-percent certain the twins were his biological daughters. Hazel had moved out after picking a huge fight and didn't come home for a month. She'd said she needed time and space to clear her head and decide if being married was the right thing for her. What she meant was being married to *him*. Since she didn't go home to her parents' house or stay with her sister, he'd suspected and she'd confirmed she'd gone back to the musician boyfriend with whom she'd been in a relationship before the two of them met.

The timing of the pregnancy caused him to doubt he was their father, which didn't make him love the twins any less. He'd been ready to talk to Hazel about his concern once they got through the pregnancy and those early months. It had taken him a minute to do the math. Twins came early, Hazel had said. It wasn't unusual.

Darren had committed to his marriage. When Hazel came home, they'd talked and agreed to go the distance with each other, just like in their vows. He'd never wavered from his promise despite the fact that he loved his wife, but wasn't wildly in love with her like he'd been with…

He wouldn't go there.

After the girls were born, they were knee-deep in dirty diapers. A paternity test needed to happen, but he kept putting it off, trying to figure out the best time to spring the news on Hazel. Things between them had been going good and he hadn't wanted to stir the pot. Except the niggling voice in the back of his mind kept reminding him it wouldn't be fair to the girls or their biological father if they weren't his to stay in the dark.

Before he could bring up the subject to Hazel, she was gone. And then he was a single father with only a suspicion she'd cheated while they lived apart.

A year had passed by in a flash with the girls after their mother's death. Suddenly, they were eighteen months and he still hadn't taken the damn test.

Once Hazel died, her parents had come close to threatening to take the girls. They'd tap-danced on a line that shouldn't be crossed.

They seemed to realize cooperation was in the girls' best interest all the way around. Stacie had stepped in to defend him and help bring reason to an overcharged emotional mess.

*They'd* been a mess. But then, they'd lost their baby girl, so he couldn't fault them too much even if he'd been the one to take the brunt of their anger.

Apologies had been made and he'd forgiven them for the sake of the girls. They needed grandparents, and his folks were gone. They needed an aunt, and he had no siblings. And they needed their father, which had been him every step of the way.

Like they say, "if it ain't broke, don't fix it." But he didn't feel good about not knowing the truth. Plus, his math could have been off, the girls could have been

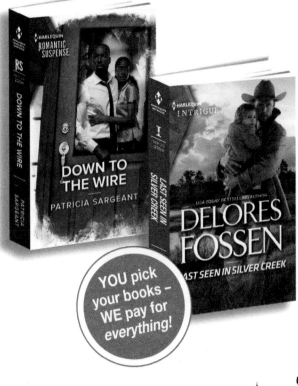

Dear Reader,

Your opinions are important to us. So if you'll participate in our fast and free "One Minute" Survey, YOU can pick up to four wonderful books that WE pay for when you try the Harlequin Reader Service!

As a leading publisher of women's fiction, we'd love to hear from you. That's why we promise to reward you for completing our survey.

IMPORTANT: Please complete the survey and return it. We'll send your Free Books and a Free Mystery Gift right away. And we pay for shipping and handling too!  *We pay for EVERYTHING!*

Try **Harlequin® Romantic Suspense** and get 2 books featuring heart-racing page-turners with unexpected plot twists and irresistible chemistry that will keep you guessing to the very end.

Try **Harlequin Intrigue® Larger-Print** and get 2 books featuring action-packed stories that will keep you on the edge of your seat. Solve the crime and deliver justice at all costs.

**Or TRY BOTH!**

Thank you again for participating in our "One Minute" Survey. It really takes just a minute (or less) to complete the survey... and your free books and gift will be well worth it!

If you continue with your subscription, you can look forward to curated monthly shipments of brand-new books from your selected series, always at a discount off the cover price! Plus you can cancel any time. So don't miss out, return your One Minute Survey today to get your Free books.

*Pam Powers*

# "One Minute" Survey

## GET YOUR FREE BOOKS AND A FREE GIFT!

✓ Complete this Survey ✓ Return this survey

◄ DETACH AND MAIL CARD TODAY! ▼

**1** Do you try to find time to read every day?
☐ YES ☐ NO

**2** Do you prefer stories with suspensful storylines?
☐ YES ☐ NO

**3** Do you enjoy having books delivered to your home?
☐ YES ☐ NO

**4** Do you share your favorite books with friends?
☐ YES ☐ NO

**YES!** I have completed the above "One Minute" Survey. Please send me my Free Books and a Free Mystery Gift (worth over $20 retail). I understand that I am under no obligation to buy anything, as explained on the back of this card.

☐ **Harlequin® Romantic Suspense** 240/340 CTI G2AD

☐ **Harlequin Intrigue® Larger-Print** 199/399 CTI G2AD

☐ **BOTH** 240/340 & 199/399 CTI G2AE

| | |
|---|---|
| FIRST NAME | LAST NAME |

ADDRESS

| | |
|---|---|
| APT.# | CITY |

| | |
|---|---|
| STATE/PROV. | ZIP/POSTAL CODE |

EMAIL ☐ Please check this box if you would like to receive newsletters and promotional emails from Harlequin Enterprises ULC and its affiliates. You can unsubscribe anytime.

© 2023 HARLEQUIN ENTERPRISES ULC
® and ™ are trademarks owned by Harlequin Enterprises ULC. Printed in the U.S.A.

HI/HRS-1123-OM

**❖HARLEQUIN** Reader Service —**Here's how it works:**

Accepting your 2 free books and free gift (gift valued at approximately $10.00 retail) places you under no obligation to buy anything. You may keep the books and gift and return the shipping statement marked "cancel." If you do not cancel, approximately one month later we'll send you more books from the series you have chosen, and bill you at our low, subscribers-only discount price. Harlequin® Romantic Suspense books consist of 4 books each month and cost just $5.99 each in the U.S. or $6.74 each in Canada, a savings of at least 8% off the cover price. Harlequin Intrigue® Larger-Print books consist of 6 books each month and cost just $6.99 each in the U.S. or $7.49 each in Canada, a savings of at least 10% off the cover price. It's quite a bargain! Shipping and handling is just 50¢ per book in the U.S. and $1.25 per book in Canada*. You may return any shipment at our expense and cancel at any time by contacting customer service — or you may continue to receive monthly shipments at our low, subscribers-only discount price plus shipping and handling.

that early and he could be stressing for literally no reason. Confirmation would be a good thing.

He couldn't ask Stacie for advice, considering she had no idea he was even questioning paternity. Could he ask Reese? She was objective. She could keep a secret. And yet, risking telling anyone else gave him chest pains.

He'd think about it.

"Darren?" his mother-in-law, Alice, said, sounding a little perturbed.

"Yes," he said, realizing he'd zoned out on their conversation.

"Do you want me to put the girls on the phone?" she asked but one of the babies picked that moment to belt out a good cry. "Oh, no. I better go."

"I'll call back later," he promised. Stopping by with Reese might not be his best play, especially after the way Stacie had reacted to her being in his home yesterday. Was Reese right? Did Stacie want more than to be the girls' aunt?

The situation was a potential powder keg. Just like paternity.

Alice ended the call before he could say goodbye or ask about the past.

He walked in and then handed his cell over to Reese, who traded rooms.

"How'd it go?" he asked, hoping she got more than he did when she returned after a couple of minutes.

"It was so long ago that she doesn't remember much," Reese said. "She set up a group chat, though, and is putting the question out to my siblings and

Granny. I explained what happened to me, briefly, and reassured her that I'm fine."

"Good," he said.

"I didn't want word to get out and them to hear the news from someone else," she explained. "I also asked if they'd been expecting me and she said they were at some point soon but I didn't give an exact day."

He nodded.

"Wait a second," he said. "Granny is on the group chat? I thought she hated technology."

"Me, too," she agreed. "But then, a lot has probably changed in a decade."

He nodded. Hell, his life looked nothing like it had two and a half years ago, when he'd been newly married. The marriage happened after a whirlwind courtship and, to be honest, he'd had doubts about what they'd done, too. So he couldn't blame Hazel. She'd had doubts. His had to have been written all over his face, if not his actions.

"Anyway, maybe we'll get a few responses," she continued. "So much time has passed. I can see why cold cases become harder and harder to solve."

"Hell, I forget what I ate for breakfast yesterday, let alone try to recall anything but generalizations from a traumatic event that happened more than a decade ago," he said.

"True."

Darren fixed another cup of coffee, turned around and leaned his hip against the counter. The paternity test was on his mind, and he could use another opinion. Someone who didn't have anything to lose or gain from the outcome would be ideal. Could he trust Reese?

He studied her for a long moment, then decided to throw it out there, for better or worse after shooting a warning look. "Can I ask you a question?"

# Chapter Thirteen

The seriousness in Darren's tone had Reese grabbing hold of the back of a chair to steady herself. "Absolutely. Ask anything." She had no idea where this was going but prepared herself for something deeply personal.

He stared at her for a long moment. After a deep sigh, he said, "First of all, this stays between you and me. I need your word."

After everything they'd been through, she was honored that he would trust her again. "You have it. Whatever you tell me never leaves this room."

He nodded as his lips pressed into a frown. Whatever was coming was going to be big based on how long it was taking him to get to the point. "There is a question as to whether or not I'm the biological father of the twins."

This was a bombshell she never would have expected in a million years. She needed to take her time to formulate a response, because he didn't need to be judged for whatever had happened in his marriage. She could also see why he couldn't talk to anyone else about this. His own parents were gone and he had no siblings. Stacie would most likely freak out and her parents might hire a fancy lawyer and file for custody.

"Have you thought about taking a test?" she asked, then realized he would have thought of that first. She held up a hand. "Forget I asked that. Of course, you have."

"Over and over again." He explained the situation with Hazel, and why he suspected the girls might not belong to him. "I'm at the point with them now that we've gotten through the first year without their mother, which, believe me, there were moments when I didn't think any of us would survive from lack of sleep."

"There wasn't a choice because you would never let them down," she pointed out. "It's easy to see that you would do anything for those girls. Period."

He nodded with a look of appreciation. "There was no way I was going to let those girls suffer in any way."

"It's also a big part of the reason that you put up with their aunt," she said. "You try to see the best in her because you need to keep her close for their sake."

"I won't argue that point even though I never really think about it," he admitted.

"When do you have time?" she asked. "You've been in survival mode for the past year. I can see it in your eyes."

Her comment might have gone too far and been too personal because he dropped his gaze to study the rim of his coffee mug. "That's a fair assessment."

She was relieved that he wasn't upset by the comment. Before she'd disappeared, they had been able to have honest conversations. Not only was he a boyfriend, but he had also been her other best friend.

"You're doing a great job with them, by the way," she added.

His gaze came up to meet hers as he cocked an eyebrow. "How do you know?"

"Kids need unconditional love," she pointed out. "Food, yes. Shelter, yes. Those basics are important, but love trumps all."

"They have that," he said and then dropped his gaze again. "But what if they're not mine, Reese?"

"You'll deal with it when it comes," she said. "Surely Stacie and her parents would agree that you are the best person for the job in bringing up those babies."

"I'm not so sure about that," he admitted with a frown. "They almost fought me for custody after Hazel's death. The only reason they decided to back off was because they had no real grounds and I think they realized their actions would put an unnecessary strain on our relationship and damage it beyond repair."

"Well, they would have been making a huge mistake," she said. "You're great for those children."

"I hope so," he said. "It's what Hazel would have wanted if she'd been able to speak up. Whether they were mine or not, she chose me as their father. She had to have done the math. She lied to me about how far along she was."

"You didn't go to any doctor appointments?" she asked.

He shook his head. "You know what work is like on a cattle ranch, even a small operation like mine. I have one ranch hand who does what I can't. He comes and takes care of my horse out back on his way to and from work so I can focus on the girls. Bradley is my lifeline."

"I'm guessing Hazel encouraged you to work so she could cover up the lie," she said.

"There was only a few weeks difference, so she probably figured she could keep me in the dark as long as I didn't show up and ask questions," he said. "She said everything was going fine and that she wanted me to save days off for when the babies made their appearance." He shook his head. "I should have been there for her and then she wouldn't have felt the need to lie."

"It might have been denial on her part or wishful thinking," she advised. It wasn't unusual for someone to hide from a scary truth until they couldn't any longer. "Did you have a conversation with her before she—"

"No," he interjected before she could finish her sentence—a sentence she didn't want to finish. "Because her death was unexpected. I'd like to believe she would have handled things differently if she'd known that day would have been her last."

"I'm sure," she observed. "You two were on a good footing and building a life together. She might not have wanted to believe the twins could be anyone else's."

"Part of the reason she and the musician broke up

before we met was because he wasn't the settling-down type," he explained. "He was honest about it with her. Said he would be devoted to her but no marriage or children."

The way he said the last part stung because it hit a little too close to home.

"I have to believe Hazel chose the person she wanted to be with for the long haul, Darren. She chose you to be the one to bring up the twins with, and I know you—once you made a commitment to someone, you wouldn't go back on it."

"I took my vows seriously," he said before taking a sip of coffee.

"Bringing up those girls is no different," she said. "Even if they aren't yours biologically, Hazel chose you and her parents will respect her wish."

Darren took a lap around the kitchen. "I keep thinking this jerk deserves to know he has children if they don't turn out to be mine and they are his."

"You know who he is?" she asked.

"I have a name, and I searched online to see who he was," he admitted. "Never wanted to know anything more about him than was absolutely necessary. Besides, she said she went to see the musician when she was gone for the month. I assumed it was him, especially after the way she talked about him when we first got together and discussed our pasts."

"I agree on some level that he deserves to know if he turns out to be the father, but maybe focus on one step at a time," she said. "Take the test for yourself and then decide what to do from there based on the result. Not doing anything is always an option. Hazel made a choice. She hid the truth for what I'm sure were good reasons. Even if they weren't, they were *her* reasons and we'll never know what they were."

"Respecting her wishes is important to me," he admitted. "But maybe you're right. Maybe I'm worried over nothing."

"I'll stay right here while you take the test if you'd like," she offered. "And I won't tell a soul about this conversation. I swear on my father's grave."

Darren took in a deep breath and then exhaled. "Okay. I'll take the test."

"Can I use your laptop?" she asked.

He nodded, so she walked over and searched for a nearby lab. There was one half an hour drive from here that could use a hair sample.

"All we need is eight strands of hair and we can drop off the samples at the lab. It's only thirty minutes out of our way," she said.

"How long before the results come back?" he asked.

"You're looking at a maximum of three days." She lifted her gaze from the screen to his face. "All I need is a ziplock bag and the samples to make it happen. Are you in?"

Darren took another lap around the kitchen. He raked fingers through his hair. And then he stopped. "Okay."

Reese helped gather the supplies. The girls' hairbrush was easy enough to get samples from. The lab needed at least eight strands. Since the girls had been born with heads full of hair based on their pictures, getting enough wasn't an issue. He grabbed his own hairbrush and did the same, placing the contents in a separate baggie.

"We need to head out," she said. "Might as well drop this off on our way to see Tandra's parents."

"Let's do it," he said, then drained his cup. He'd been stressed about taking this test for so long now, it felt strangely calming to be taking action. "And thank you for helping me get my head on straight about this."

Reese walked over to him and placed a palm on the center of his chest. "You're a good man, Darren. You deserve peace of mind."

THIS CLOSE, he could see her pulse pound at the base of her throat. It matched tempo with his, which was climbing. He could also smell the citrus shampoo he kept in the guest bath, and it had never smelled sexier on someone.

He lifted his gaze to her full pink lips—lips that looked a little too tempting when her tongue slicked across the bottom one. It would be so easy to kiss her. Would she welcome his lips on hers?

His question was answered when he locked gazes and saw an equal amount of desire in those beautiful eyes of hers. "Can I kiss you right now?"

"I'd be disappointed if you didn't," she said, pushing up to her tiptoes, making access that much easier.

With her lips this close, it didn't take much to kiss. Her hands came up to his chest and grabbed fistfuls of his shirt, then she tugged him closer. He parted her lips with his tongue, and she released a sexy little moan against his mouth that caused blood to flow south.

Kissing Reese was up there on his list of his favorite things. In fact, the sparks flying between them were something he hadn't experienced since—since... Since *her*.

By the time they separated, they were both gasping for air. He smiled as he brought up the backs of his fingers to brush against her cheek.

Beautiful Reese. Dangerous Reese. Foolish him. Because this would only lead to more heartache for him when she bolted back to her life. Normally, casual sex with her would top his list of favorite things. With their history, there wouldn't be anything casual about sex.

Darren took a step back and dropped his hands to his sides. "We should get going." He could hear the gravelly quality to his own voice, so he coughed to cover. It was an unoriginal move, but his head wasn't exactly on straight right now, or he never would stoked his desire with that kiss. Because it had him wanting more and Reese had limits—limits that would have her running for the hills if they got too close.

And he needed that heartache like he needed a hole in the head.

Besides, all his attention had to go to his girls right now. He could date casually, dip his toe in the water, but he couldn't afford to get attached to anyone again. Especially now that he was committed to taking the paternity test. The results could add ammunition to a court case, but he vowed right then and there to fight for custody with everything he had if his former parents-in-law decided to challenge parental rights. His bank account was no match for their money. They could afford to hire the best attorney—an attorney who could run circles around him in court.

A noise sounded outside, in back. Normally, that wouldn't register as alarming.

Darren locked gazes with Reese. "Stay away from windows and doors while I check this out, okay?"

Eyes wide, she nodded. And then immediately crossed the room to grab a knife. Darren kept a shotgun in the hall closet with a box of shells on the top shelf, far out of reach of little hands. He grabbed both and loaded a pair of slugs.

Armed and ready with his finger hovering over the trigger mechanism, he slipped out the front door. Reese had the presence of mind to lock it behind him. Good. He realized a few seconds too late that he should have told her to, but she was on it.

Back against the house, he raised the shotgun barrel toward the sky before rounding the first corner. Adrenaline pumped so hard that blood rushed in his ears, making it difficult for him to hear.

Taking the first corner, he moved fast and lowered the barrel. He scanned the area. No sign of anyone. Without hesitating, he kept going until he could see the backyard. Out of the corner of his eye, he saw movement.

Darren bolted toward the male figure who was running fast and hard. Pumping his legs until his thighs burned, Darren did his best to catch up to the bastard who'd been in his backyard. Iris's tricycle had been pushed up against the house, near the kitchen window. He heard the back door open and assumed Reese followed.

Anger ripped through him. The runner was fast. He disappeared into nearby trees and then the sound of a motorcycle engine firing up filled the air. Darren released a string of swear words. Whoever was after Reese could be checking his home to see if she was there or coming for him. Finding answers and talking to Tandra's family just jumped up the priority list. So did carrying a weapon at all times.

As he headed back toward the house, an explosion rocked the ground. A ringing noise filled his ears as he bolted toward the sound. Fire ravaged his small home. His cell phone was inside so he couldn't call 911.

Where was Reese?

As he neared the blaze, he called out for her.

Just as panic coiled in his chest, he saw her. She was on flat on her back with her hand over her heart, lying in the grass.

"Reese," he said as he ran toward her full speed.

She didn't move.

## Chapter Fourteen

Darren's panicked voice broke through the ringing sound in Reese's ears. She rolled onto her side, winced and coughed as he dropped down to his knees beside her.

"Hey," he said as she blinked up at him. "Where does it hurt?"

She could barely hear him. Her throat and lungs burned from smoke inhalation. Talking was next to impossible. She reached for him and grabbed on to his forearms.

"Help is on the way," he said to her. Reading lips helped her understand what he was saying. "Hang in there. Okay?"

Reese nodded. Movement hurt. Whoever the bastard was trying to erase her had another think coming. Trying to sit up was a bad idea. Moving was a bad idea. Looking into Darren's eyes and seeing his concern for her was a bad idea. That last one made her wish she'd done things differently. Since regret was nothing more than a waste of time, she pushed aside the sentiment.

"You're going to be all right," Darren soothed. His voice brought comfort even though the dark cloud feeling overhead made it feel like it would be short-lived.

"Your home," she said, managing to get the words out through a cracked, dry throat.

"I know," he said. "It's not important, though. Those are only things and things can be replaced. You're alive. You're safe. That's all that matters right now."

Because of her, his children had lost everything. The sobering thought kicked her in the teeth. She shook her head, determined to leave him out of this nightmare from now on. Plus, his former parents-in-law had threatened to fight him for custody of the girls once. How would this play out once they found out what happened here? He'd brought someone into his family's home who threatened their safety. Even though she would never do anything to put the girls in harm's way on purpose, reality seemed to have a mind of its own.

"Me being here puts your girls at risk," she said as sirens pierced through the fog in her brain.

In the next half hour, the fire was out and Reese was in the back of an ambulance on her way to the hospital. A deputy was supposed to meet them there to get statements. Darren's SUV hadn't sustained any damage and a neighbor volunteered to call in his construction crew to at least seal off the premises best as they could. Reese had an oxygen mask strapped to her face but was breathing fine. Her body was starting to ache, but nothing was broken based on the field exam. There would be bruising, no doubt. That wasn't anything she couldn't get over in a couple of days or a week depending on how bad it got. There would most definitely be a huge bruise on her right hip.

Thinking about leaving Darren caused her chest to squeeze, but it would have to be done for the sake of his family. She needed to lure whoever was trying to kill her away from the Pierce family. A thought struck. Darren would follow her if she tried to leave.

She would bang her head against the wall if it didn't hurt so much already. As it was, her brain felt like it might split in two from pain. Her hands fisted as she thought about the bastard who was after her. Had she opened a can of worms with digging into Camree Lynn's disappearance? That was the only explanation that made any sense. Why else would someone try to kill her? And then what? Make it look random? Or like she'd come across poachers yesterday?

Her thoughts shifted to Darren and the kiss that would now be the benchmark for all future kisses. He'd held the record since high school and had somehow bested himself. The grown-man version of Darren caused all kinds of sensations in her body— sensations she didn't need to focus on, considering there was no outlet for them no matter how much they sparked.

By the time the ambulance arrived at the hospital, Reese felt much better. She would argue about checking in but figured it might not hurt to have a doctor give her the all-clear just in case.

Darren's cell had been inside the house, which was now roped off as a crime scene. Or at least what was left of it. The thought of him losing everything gutted her. There had to be so many memories locked inside those walls. Memories of the girls in the form of pictures and toys. Memories of their mother. Memories of the short time they'd spent there as a family.

She was being sentimental, but those things mattered when people were building a life together. They took on a new importance when one of those people was gone. Thinking about all those little keepsakes going up in flames or being damaged by water when the firemen put out the fire, made her sick to her stomach.

The bastard responsible needed to pay.

Reese took in a deep breath as the doors opened. A few seconds later, she was being wheeled out of the ambulance and into the automatic glass doors of the ER. She went straight into a room, where Darren found her almost immediately. The look on his face was a mix of desperation, frustration and concern.

"I'm okay," she said after lifting the oxygen mask enough to speak. "I feel better already."

In the next second, he was by her side, reaching for her hand. The minute they made physical contact, she breathed a little easier. He was a lifeline in this chaos.

"I've been thinking that I must have been investigating Camree Lynn's disappearance on my way down," she said. "It's the only thing that makes sense to me as to why someone would target me."

"Just rest, okay?" He brought his free hand up to

touch her face. The way he looked at her with such admiration hit her in the center of her chest.

"I almost got you killed," she said. "Why aren't you mad at me?"

"Because it wasn't your fault," he said. "Even if you were digging into Camree Lynn's disappearance. There's no way you could have known any of this would happen. You're not the bad guy here. And I know without a shadow of a doubt that there's no way you would have brought this to my doorstep." He stopped for a second and bit down on his lower lips. Then, he seemed to say "what the hell" because he opened his mouth to speak. "I think it's safe to say that I'm the last person you wanted to see when you headed back toward Cider Creek."

"That's not exactly true," she responded. "I've wanted to reach out to you for years to apologize. But I didn't think you'd give me the time of day. And I didn't deserve it after the way I handled things, so I did you a favor and stayed away."

He stood there for a long moment, as though deciding for himself if he could believe her. Then, he gave a small nod of agreement.

"You're here now," he said after a long pause. "We've grown up. You have an important job. I have my girls and the family ranch to take care of."

"Speaking of which, will you be able to stay there now that your home is unlivable?" she asked, redirecting the conversation before he could give her a free pass.

"That's the plan," he said.

"Why don't you live there now?" she asked. "If you don't mind my asking."

"It was always my folks' place," he said. "This might not make any sense, but their memory is preserved there. I check in on the house every day while I'm on site. There's always food stocked in the kitchen, at least enough for lunches and the occasional dinner when I'm working late."

"It makes sense to me," she reassured him. "Maybe it's time to fill it again and still preserve their memory."

"A fresh start," he said.

"I think they would have enjoyed you and the girls living there and filling the halls with laughter again," she pointed out.

Could the two of them start over, too?

DARREN LIKED THE idea of his girls growing up around his mother's things. He could add a few touches of his own to make the place feel like home to them. His own home would take time to fix, even if insurance acted fast. He could fix it up and sell it, which would give him some breathing room with his finances. "It's time."

"Good," Reese said with a self-satisfied smile. She sat up a little straighter and took the oxygen mask completely off.

A loud beeping noise had her thinking she'd made a wrong move. A nurse came rushing in.

"Don't take that off unless you've been cleared," the short nurse with a name tag that read *Angela* ordered.

She couldn't be more than five-two and her tone said she was not one to be messed with. Darren didn't dare cross her, and based on the look on Reese's face, she got the message, too.

"Yes, ma'am," Reese said, replacing the mask. "I do think I've improved."

"The doctor will be in soon. He'll decide that. In the meantime, don't mess with it again," Angela scolded, wagging a finger at Reese.

Angela checked the machine and then rushed out of the room, almost running into a deputy. She fussed at him, too, until he backed up into the hallway.

"I'll go see what he wants since you already gave a statement back at my house," Darren said.

She nodded.

He smiled as he left the room.

He almost made a crack that Texas could replace its former slogan from Don't Mess with Texas to Don't Mess with Nurses.

"I can try to answer any questions you might have, Deputy Lyle," Darren said as he read the deputy's name tag. The man looked to be in his midforties. He was roughly six feet tall and could be described as sturdy.

Darren offered his hand and introduced himself. After a firm handshake, he continued, "What can I do for you?"

"I dropped by to say we're opening up an investigation into Camree Lynn's disappearance despite this being a cold case," Deputy Lyle said. "I wanted to deliver the news myself."

"I appreciate you coming all the way here," Darren said.

"My place isn't far and I'm on my way home," he explained. Then he said, "I have a fifteen-year-old daughter. She's a handful sometimes. My wife says it's hormones and that it'll calm down eventually but there are days when I doubt that's possible." His smile faded when he said, "We're in the middle of a divorce and my wife noticed the Tandra St. Clair case on the news. She went digging around and found several cases around the state that had girls missing in the midst of a divorce who'd been classified as runaways."

"I found three," Darren admitted. He noticed the deputy used the word *wife* instead of *soon to be ex-wife*. It made Darren think the divorce might not be his idea.

"She did, too," Deputy Lyle said. "Anyway, it got her pretty worked up since we've been going through a rough patch like these other families. Our daughter is in a rebellious phase and my wife started overthinking, worrying. I guess she got me riled up, too. So I talked to my boss and he said I could reopen the case."

"Reese will be relieved to hear the sheriff is actually taking this seriously," Darren said. "The trail is cold, so it won't be easy."

"No," Deputy Lyle said. "But these other cases aren't as old, and we have something new to work with to bring to a joint task force. If they're related and we have a serial killer on our hands, we have to do everything in our power to stop him."

"I appreciate you stopping by to deliver the news," Darren said.

"Local law enforcement has a lot to make up for after Sheriff Tanner's arrest," Deputy Lyle said.

The statement didn't put Darren at ease with the current situation. "I better get back in."

Deputy Lyle nodded, then shook hands and headed toward the elevator bank. Darren didn't like being away from Reese for too long. He had a bad feeling that was probably nothing.

## Chapter Fifteen

The door opened. The lights suddenly turned off, plunging the room into darkness. Reese opened her mouth to scream and then realized the oxygen mask would muffle the sound. She reached for the panic button and then remembered all she had to do was take off the mask.

As she jerked the thing off her face, she slammed her free hand into the machine next to her as she tried to scramble out of bed. Where was nurse Angela?

A hand gripped her arm as she opened her mouth to scream. An alarm sounded. The strong hand jerked her off the bed as she screamed.

Reese fisted her hands and threw punches, swinging at air. She kicked and finally connected. The male attacker grunted, and she thought it served him right. When she threw a second kick, he was smart enough to get out of the way.

He hauled her to her feet and then off the ground, so she unleashed a rampage of kicks. This time, he cursed under his breath and dropped her. Her feet hit the tile flooring too fast, too suddenly. She grasped for something to hold on to before she face-planted. Her elbow jabbed into something hard. Bone?

And then she heard whoever it was coming toward her. She readied herself for a fight, feeling around for anything she could use as a weapon.

The door opened.

"I thought I told you—"

Angela's voice was unmistakable.

"Excuse me," a deep male voice said as the light flipped on a second before he brushed past Angela and ran into the hallway.

"Stop him," Reese yelled as she scrambled to her feet.

Angela let the man brush right past her. She took one look at Reese and then turned back toward the hallway. "Stop that man!"

"Someone came into my room. I need my clothes. I'm leaving," Reese said.

Angela grabbed her cell phone out of her pocket and made a call to security as she put her free hand up to stop Reese. After making the request, she said, "Your friend is out there. What happened in here?"

"I already told you," Reese said, opening cabinets to locate the bag with her clothes inside. She distinctly remembered being given a plastic one but had no idea where it had gone.

"Did you know him?" Angela asked.

"I'm afraid I have no idea who that man was and he's the reason I'm in here in the first place," she said as Darren came barreling into the room. She made eye contact immediately. "He was here." She lifted her arm so he could see the grip marks.

"How?" Darren muttered a few choice words. "Did you get a good look at him?"

"Afraid not," Reese said as she opened the cabinet with her personal effects. "There we go. Right here. Now if you'll excuse me." She made a beeline for the attached bathroom.

Angela seemed to know better than to argue. "Security is on its way."

Reese ripped off the hospital gown and put her clothes on, then slipped into her shoes. She couldn't wait to get out of there.

Darren waited at the door, reminding her, "The nurse called Security."

"Too late," she said, staring at him. "I'm not staying here a minute longer."

"I'm sorry I left you alone," he said, then reached for her hand and linked their fingers. "This is my fault."

"You had no idea this would happen," she said.

"This bastard slipped past me when I was right down the hall." He shook his head. "I never would have forgiven myself if something had happened to you."

"You have been sticking your neck out and putting your life on the line for me since I showed up on your property," she insisted. "You've done nothing wrong except try to help. If anyone is sorry, it's me. It's my fault your house is burned down. All your memories are gone."

Tucking her chin to her chest, she stifled a sniffle.

"Let's get out of here and then we can clear the air," he said, lifting her chin up until her gaze met his again. "Deal?"

She nodded. "I'm ready."

As they turned toward the door, it burst open. The deputy stopped in the door jamb, panting. "He got away. Any chance you got a good look at his face?"

"No," Reese admitted. "And I have no plans to stay here for him to finish the job, security or not."

She gave a quick rundown of what happened.

"How can I reach you?" the deputy asked.

"My cell burned beyond usage," Darren said.

Deputy Lyle produced a business card. "Once you get a working cell, program this number in."

Darren took the offering. "Will do."

"I'm taking her home," Darren said. "To Pierce Ranch."

"I believe I know where that is," Deputy Lyle said.

"If you are inclined to drive past it every now and then, it wouldn't hurt either of our feelings," Darren stated.

"It definitely wouldn't hurt mine," Reese added.

"Will do," Deputy Lyle said before escorting them to Darren's SUV. They arrived safely despite the bad feeling Reese had while walking through the parking lot. The hairs on the back of her neck pricked, which was never a good sign. Of course, at this point, she might be spooked and freaking out. But still. She had no plans to take chances.

Darren helped her into the passenger side of his SUV. The second the door was closed, she got a whiff of smoke. As soon as he claimed the driver's seat and turned on the engine, she cracked the window.

"You might want to crack the other windows, too," she said. "I didn't realize how badly these clothes smelled of smoke."

He nodded, then pulled forward out of the parking spot. Before he got too far, he hit the buttons to lower all the windows a little. "How's your head?"

"I have a monster headache but that doesn't seem to be anything new," she said.

"The guy back there," he continued after a moment of silence. "Did you get anything from him? A general build?"

"He wasn't big like you," she said. "I only saw him for a flash, but he looked slightly average height and build." Average for Texans in this area was six feet tall. "He was strong. His grip strength caught me off guard. He had grabby hands."

"Did he say anything?" Darren asked after the muscle in his jaw clenched. "Did you hear his voice at all?"

"Not really," she said. "When the nurse walked back in, he mumbled but I couldn't get a clear take on his voice."

"The person responsible for the fire at my house must have stuck around to watch the rest unfold," Darren said.

"I didn't think about that before, but you're right," she said.

"He might know my property if he knows the equipment building," he continued. "Which means he might be local or someone who grew up around here."

"Phillip Rhodes spent summers here for years, even after the camp closed," she said.

"I'm almost thinking this person had to have grown up around here at this point despite the fact taking someone so close to home would draw attention," Darren said. "Camree Lynn's case was a long time ago. She might have been where he started."

"So you're leaning toward Aiden Archer?" she asked.

He nodded. "That seems to be the best name so far."

It had been a long time since she'd been to Darren's family home. A whole lot of good memories were stored there. Memories of going to his place after school to do homework, and stealing a few kisses when his mother wasn't looking. They'd held hands under the stars while sitting on the tire swing in his backyard. Her thoughts were flooded with good memories as he pulled onto ranch property.

Reminiscing about the past was a good distraction from what had just happened to her. Another attack and they were further from answers than this morning. How could this person act alone? How would a single person have pulled off what happened at the equipment building? She could have sworn she'd heard more than one voice.

Then again, she'd been pretty out of it. The blow to her head might have caused her to mix up details.

At least her head had been spared the floor at the

hospital. And yet, nausea was still settling in as a monster headache formed. Thinking hurt.

DARREN PARKED IN the detached garage and then came around to the passenger side. He needed to do something about the lack of a cell phone. Being disconnected from his girls for the day caused a coil to tighten in his chest. Ever since their mother died, he'd worried something would happen to them. Like, maybe, he was cursed.

But the girls were thriving and, so far, hadn't met any accidents that didn't involve potty training.

"I need a phone," he said to Reese.

"We should have stopped along the way and gotten one of those throw-away phones. They come with service," she said. "I don't think they cost much."

"Can you make it to the store?" he asked.

"I don't want to stay here by myself," she said.

"Okay," he confirmed. "To the store we go." And then he stopped. "When we get back, we'll fill Buster in. He'll be sleeping in the bunkhouse."

"Buster still works for your family ranch?" she asked.

"That's right," he confirmed. He was also thinking it would be good to have another set of eyes around. Someone who could keep an eye out for danger. There were no security alarms in his parents' home, so all they had to work with would be door locks. He was seeing how easily the bastard targeting Reese was able to move through the hospital. It wasn't exactly reassuring how stealthy this guy could be.

"I'd love to see him and say hello," she said. And then she seemed to think better of it. "Unless he doesn't want to see me again."

"He'll be happy you turned up," he said. He held back the part about how many times Buster had asked when Reese was coming around again, or if Darren had called her to let her know how he felt before she got mixed up with his uncle.

Darren had been stubborn back then, digging his heels in. Some might say little had changed, but he would argue differently. Now that the girls were here, he'd learned to relax and cut back on his stubborn side. Especially as they started having ideas of their own, like when they wanted to be held and when they wanted to walk. It seemed the minute they learned they could move across the room without his help, they'd decided to do things on their own. Was it a sign of what was to come in the future? Probably. As much as he wanted to bring up strong young ladies, a piece of his heart would always want them to need their daddy.

By the time Darren drove them to the store and back, another hour had passed. Reese napped on the way. When he pulled up next to the farmhouse where he'd grown up, he parked the SUV and then touched her arm.

"Hey, we're here," he said quietly.

"Home?" Reese asked in a sleepy voice that tugged at his heart. Letting that voice penetrate the walls he'd built around his heart to survive would be just plain foolish of him. Determined not to make the same mistake twice, he shelved his emotions.

"We're at the farmhouse," he said, thinking how weird it was going to be to call this place home. Then again, he was warming up to the idea of his children growing up here. Being around their grandmother and grandfather's things was the next best thing to being around them.

"Okay," she said, wiping her eyes. "Right. Are you going to see Buster?"

"I'll have him swing by," he said. "Looks like you need your rest."

"I'm good," she promised.

"You've been through a lot, Reese," he reasoned. "You're tired and need sleep. I'll be right here."

"But Tandra was the most recent and she might be out there in danger," she argued. "What if we can save her?"

Darren looked at Reese. "I'll make calls. It will be faster to do it that way, anyway. We won't lose time driving around."

Reese looked like she was about to put up an argument.

"I have this throwaway and I'll find numbers from the internet," he said. There was a desktop computer in the office that he could use.

She nodded.

He exited the driver's side and moved around the front of the SUV, then opened the door for her and helped her out.

"This place brings back a lot of memories," she said with a small smile.

"Sure does," he agreed. This was also the place where his heart had been shattered to bits, but he was certain she wasn't talking about that particular memory.

Bringing her here might be a mistake but he was short on options. Making those calls might bring answers.

## Chapter Sixteen

Reese walked inside the house on her own, but her legs felt like they were made of rubber bands instead of bone. "I can't wait to get out of these clothes. Is there anything else I can wear?"

Darren nodded. He'd become quiet and she couldn't help but wonder what was going through his mind. Being back in this house with him brought back a flood of memories. They were good. They reminded her of why she'd fallen for Darren. Maybe that was the reason he looked so grim. Maybe he didn't want any of those memories.

Darren excused himself and returned holding out what looked like a complete outfit. "You left these here once when we fell into the pond."

"I wondered where these warm-ups went," she said. "These were my favorites." Thank the stars for the small miracle of a sports bra and underwear with the offering.

"You always kept them in your backpack on Fridays for when you came over and then we fell into that stagnant water out on the property, so we threw them into the washer and forgot about them," he said.

"Cool." The memory tapped into feelings she'd tried to suppress a long time ago. She nodded and smiled. "Mind if I grab a shower?"

"Not at all," Darren said, but he was already programming a number into his cell phone. "I'll check on the girls and be in my dad's old... *My* office."

"Sounds good," she said, starting for the stairs.

"You might want to use the master," he said, motioning toward the hallway where he was headed. "I don't keep the upstairs stocked since no one lives here. I only keep towels and supplies downstairs for the occasional shower that needs to happen here before I head home."

Reese did an about-face and walked to the hallway where he was standing. He waited for her to go first. Him being in a room two doors down was a comforting thought after being attacked in the hospital. She made a mental note to call the sheriff to see what he found out on her phone records. She'd given him permission to check into her communication. Maybe he'd found something.

After the shower, Reese was beginning to feel human again. It was beyond good to get those smoky clothes off her skin. She couldn't help but think someone was desperate. Maybe their desperation would cause them to make a mistake and reveal their identity. She still had no idea who it was or why. That wasn't completely true. They had two names to start with. By the time she finished dressing and headed into the office, Darren might have an idea of which name to follow through on.

Darren was on a phone call while she stopped at the door. His body language was tense as he glanced up at her. The look on his face said he was being chewed out, or worse. The fire must have had his in-laws riled up.

"I know how to keep my own children safe," he said into the phone in a quietly controlled voice that signaled he was on the verge of losing it. He couldn't afford to lose his temper right now. It would only make matters worse given the situation.

Reese walked in, squatted beside him and took his free hand. She gave a squeeze for reassurance that he appeared to appreciate, as he gave a small nod of acknowledgement. More importantly, he didn't let go.

"I'm moving into the farmhouse," he said. "I appreciate your offer but we have a home here. It's something I've been meaning to do, anyway. This pushes up my time line."

Darren paused.

Then he said, "I appreciate your concern. I know how much you love the girls." Another few beats of silence passed before he said, "They're all I have left of her, too."

Reese could scarcely imagine what Darren had been going through since figuring out those girls might not be biologically his. Their samples went up in flames, so they would have to regroup. Giving him a definitive answer was as important to her as being there for him when he found out the news.

It was the least she could do to make up for at least some of the pain she'd caused him in the past. Maybe make a dent? Her guilt would last forever.

"I can swing by and pick them up anytime," he said into the phone. "Are you sure?" He paused a couple of beats. "Tomorrow at lunch. That'll give me time to get settled here. Sounds good."

He released her hand to push the end-call button. And then he set the phone on top of the desk and raked his fingers through his thick hair.

"What can I do to help prepare for the girls?" Reese asked, getting a second wind after her shower. "Diapers? Wipes?"

"I'll have to grab the portable cribs from the hall closet," he said. "There should be enough supplies here to last a couple of days."

"Then, we'll have time for a delivery," she said. "All we have to do is one-click our way into all the supplies you could possibly need."

"One-click is a little slower out here, but you're right about having enough to tide us over," he said. She liked the way he used the word *us*. She hoped he would let her roll her sleeves up and help. Then, it dawned on her that the fire might not be the only objection they had about him taking the girls back. "They know about me, don't they?"

He nodded.

"They're not happy about another woman being in your life," she said.

"No. They are not."

"Do they know that I'm only here temporarily?" she asked.

"They don't need to know every detail of my life," he countered. "I already tell them everything I can think of about the girls on an almost daily basis."

That couldn't be going over very well. "You always had an independent streak a mile long."

"Not when you have babies that have to come first," he said.

"They're lucky to have such a devoted father," she reminded him. He seemed to need the reminder. She would tell him that every day until he no longer needed to hear it.

"Thank you," he said. "It means a lot to hear those words."

He might not want to hear this, but, "If you feel stuck between a rock and a hard place about taking your girls or helping me, you know I understand you have to choose them."

"I do," he said, but the hint of gratitude in his voice said he appreciated her for saying it. He was taking care of twins, managing his former in-laws, and emotionally supporting his former sister-in-law while running his family's cattle ranch. Who took care of him?

"I might not be much in the kitchen, but I can dig around in there for food while you make an online order and set up the cribs," she said. "Did you call Buster?"

"I did," Darren acknowledged. "He's wrapping something up and will be on his way shortly."

Buster had always been like a big brother or uncle

to her. "I'm glad he's still here helping the ranch run smoothly."

"I don't know if I'd call it running smoothly with me at the helm, but I'm doing my best," Darren said before making eyes that finally broke some of the tension.

"The place is still going," she said. "Sounds like success to me."

"The insurance money from the house will help. I've been running two places and it has been a drain. This is a small operation and can use a cash infusion."

Reese had a little money saved. She would offer her savings if it would help, but doubted he would take her up on it. "The ranch is solvent, right?"

"That it is," he answered.

"Like I said…success."

He smiled and nodded as she left the room and headed toward the kitchen. She wasn't kidding about her cooking skills. However, she'd managed to keep herself fed and she had a few tricks up her sleeve.

In the pantry, there were cans of pinto beans and boxes of boil-in-a-bag rice. This was right up her alley. In the fridge, she located a white onion and a nice spicy sausage. She pulled out a couple of pans and got busy. First, she chopped the onion and sliced the sausage. She threw those into a saucepan with a can of pinto beans. Next, she boiled water for the rice. Fixing a meal took less than twenty minutes. Pride filled her chest at what she'd accomplished because it actually smelled good. She located two serving bowls, using one for the rice and the other for the sausage and beans.

After grabbing a couple of glasses, she filled them with water and then put on a pot of coffee like she'd down countless times after school when they'd come here to do homework, because she didn't want to risk running into Duncan. Disappearing was the best way to fly underneath his radar, and she'd been good at it.

Had she become too good at disappearing?

DARREN MADE A couple of phone calls. Tandra's family didn't answer, so he left a message. If it wasn't necessary, he wouldn't bother them at all. But he might just be able to help find their missing daughter and connect a criminal to a couple other cases, so it was worth the intrusion.

Aiden Archer was more difficult to pin down. If he was around town at all, Buster would probably know something. He'd lived here for years and knew most of the families, if not personally than by association or reputation.

Phillip Rhodes, as it turned out, worked for a major distribution chain as a delivery driver, according to his mother. He went from house to house delivering packages and had moved three times in the past five years. There were five missing teens altogether, including the additional three cases that seemed connected to Camree Lynn and Tandra. He was on shift in Barrel City, which was a two-hour drive from the farmhouse, and he clocked out at midnight this evening. They could confront him and see what he had to say. His voice might be familiar to Reese, and could possibly jar a memory.

Or he could take one look at her, panic, and assume he was busted. He could run and that would tell them everything they needed to know about his innocence. But then what? Because it would also tip their hands. There would be no sheriff with them. Was it possible to get a current picture of Rhodes to show to Reese? Maybe on social media? Would that have the same effect? It was worth a try. He might have changed a lot over the years.

Darren performed a quick social media scan. He found several listings for Phillip Rhodes on the most popular platform. A few had actual faces attached. The others had pictures or memes. He scanned a couple to see if they gave away any details of where the person might work and didn't find anything related to delivery drivers. Of course, it stood to reason a man guilty of stalking, luring, kidnapping, and possibly killing teenaged girls with trouble at home wouldn't use his real photo.

And, a creep who preyed on teenage girls might be good at hiding. It dawned on Darren how easy it would be to find out intimate information about these targets online. So many shared too many details of their private lives, making it easier for someone to lurk. The bastard could become so familiar with the target, he believed they were in a relationship.

It also occurred to him someone like Rhodes could deliver gifts if the girls were home. Of course, it would be easy to trace if the interactions occurred on the computer. Law enforcement would certainly look there first.

The common thread of troubled teens bothered Darren. The parents fighting and talking about divorce could throw off the most grounded teen. Camree Lynn had withdrawn from everyone but Reese, and Reese's guilt must have crushed her at times that she couldn't save her friend. Young people had a habit of blaming themselves for everything that happened. He should know. He'd been just as bad.

Whatever was happening in the kitchen smelled good. Hunger pulled him out of the office, and he walked toward the scent. "I thought you said you couldn't cook."

"I said that I can survive in the kitchen," Reese said with a laugh. "I wouldn't call it cooking."

Seeing her standing there in what had been her favorite warm-ups wasn't helping him with the whole keep-her-at-arm's-length plan. Fresh from the shower, her hair still wet, he could already smell her clean, citrusy scent as he walked toward the table. The eat-in round table was set for two. There were serving bowls and plates. She'd even located a candle. He shouldn't be surprised. She'd spent plenty of time here when they were young, and nothing had changed. He hadn't touched any of his mother's stuff or rearranged any of the cabinets. When he ate here, it was usually off of a paper plate or fast-food carton. His mother would have had a fit. She despised fast food, but then she kept a garden of fresh vegetables and herbs. It was easy enough for her to walk outside and grab what she needed. Everything she'd touched grew. Having a green thumb was only part of the equation. There were people who made everyone and everything else thrive around them. She'd been one of those people. They used to joke she could touch a dying tree and it would come back to life. He imagined she had a huge garden and spent her days where she was happiest.

"I put on coffee but thought you should probably drink water with your meal," Reese said.

He walked over to her before taking a seat. He'd almost lost her today to whoever had attacked her at the hospital, right under his nose. So, yeah, he knew about guilt. As it turned out, some things from childhood don't change all that much.

"I should have stayed in the room with you," he said to her.

"There was a deputy with you," she said. "This guy is brazen."

"Or desperate," he responded.

"Point taken." She bit her bottom lip. "Either way, he won't catch us off guard again."

Darren leaned forward, close enough to rest his forehead against hers. "What if I'd lost you again?"

"You won't," she said. Those words shouldn't have warmed him as much as they did.

"I can't," he said, unsure how wise the statement was under the circumstances. It covered more than the bastard who was after her. And yet, he had no idea if he could, or should, try to open his heart, even a little.

## Chapter Seventeen

With Darren standing so close, it would be easy to reach out and touch him. So Reese did. She grabbed a fistful of his shirt and held her hand against his chest. The feel of his rapid heartbeat against her fingers reminded her they were both very alive.

"I can't even think about anything happening to you, especially on my watch," Darren said against her lips.

Taking what she wanted, Reese pressed her mouth to his. A knock sounded at the back door, startling her. She took a step back.

"That must be Buster," Darren said as someone put a key in the lock mechanism. "He still knocks first even though he has a key."

"Should I set another plate?" She immediately turned toward the cabinet so Buster wouldn't see the flush to her cheeks.

"We can ask but he usually turns me down," he said.

Buster entered the room, then closed and locked the door behind him. Clearly, he was in the loop on what had been going on. His gaze moved from Darren to Reese. Buster was in his mid-to-late sixties. His skin was sun worn, his hair as black as night. Wise, pale blue eyes studied her with compassion. "It's good to see you here, Reese."

With that, he walked straight over to her and brought her into a hug. He smelled like leather and hay, with a dash of spice.

"It's really good to see you again, Buster." A tear escaped and rolled down her cheek before she could suppress it. She tucked her chin to her chest when more broke free, and sniffled. "Are you hungry?" Reese immediately turned away from him.

"Nah," Buster said.

"Thank you for taking care of the house," Darren said to Buster after a bear hug.

"I'm relieved the girls weren't there," Buster said. He had a gun tucked into a holster in the back of his jeans. Was that new? She didn't remember him carrying before. Then again, Darren's mother wasn't the type to allow a loaded gun inside her home. "Where are they now?"

"With their grandparents," Darren answered.

"Is this the longest you've gone without seeing them?" Buster asked.

Darren nodded. "They're coming home at noon tomorrow. And by home, I mean we're moving back here. It's time."

"Yes, it is," Buster agreed with a broad smile. "Your folks would be pleased, if you don't mind my saying so."

"It means a lot coming from you," Darren said.

His comment pleased Buster, based on the smile on his face.

"Are you sure you're not hungry?" Reese asked.

"I just ate before I came," he said. "But, please, sit down and eat your meal before it gets cold."

"There's fresh coffee," Reese added. That got Buster's attention and approval. He walked over to the cabinet, grabbed a mug and then poured himself a cup before turning around and leaning against the bullnose edge of the counter.

Reese and Darren took a seat at the table and passed around the bowls. The food was good if she did say so herself. Simple but tasty. It reminded her of home, because this happened to be something her mother would throw in the Crock-Pot and let simmer on low for hours, filling the house with good smells.

Funny, she'd forgotten all about the food. Why was it so easy to remember every harsh word spoken and so easy to forget all the really good stuff, like Christmases around the tree in the living room? Baking cookies for half the afternoon on Christmas Eve while her mother's favorite holiday movie played in the background. *It's a Wonderful Life* was a staple during the holidays. As were *Elf* and *The Grinch Who Stole Christmas*.

It was probably the fact that it was December that had her feeling nostalgic. But she was happy to find so many good memories tucked in the back of her mind. Maybe it was time they came to the forefront, rather than replaying all those fights she'd overheard with Duncan and her siblings. Reese knew better than to go head-to-head with the man, especially after he'd methodically run off every last one of her siblings. Now that she knew the truth, she might never forgive him for breaking up the family and causing her mother so much pain.

"What do you know about Aiden Archer?" Darren finally asked Buster.

"Not too much," he said, pressing his lips together while he seemed to be reaching deep into his thoughts. "The Archers were a tight-knit bunch—none of them were to my liking."

"Are they jerks or criminals?" Darren asked.

"Can't say that I would put anything past them," Buster concluded. "I don't know of anything in particular, but I steer clear of the family."

It was quite a statement if Buster didn't like them. He had a keen eye for judging folks. Said it came from years of sizing up young men for hiring purposes. She remembered him always talking about the eyes. All Buster had to do was look someone in the eyes and he could tell if they were bad.

The fact that he didn't care for the Archer family spoke volumes in her book. Aiden Archer topped her list at the moment.

"I didn't get a chance to update you on Phillip Rhodes yet," Darren said to her. Her stomach twisted in a knot at hearing the name. "He works for a delivery service and has moved around. He delivers packages to residential areas."

How easy would it be for him to stalk someone on his route? Especially if it changed every day. "That's convenient and fits the profile of the person responsible. Is that how you think he finds his victims?"

"He could work from the names on packages and then find the teens on their social media accounts," he mused.

"That's true," she agreed. Reese took a moment to let the news sink in. Rhodes could be exactly who they were looking for. She shivered thinking about it. Camree Lynn would have known him despite not caring for him. At least, that's what she'd said when Reese warned her friend to stay away from the man. Did Camree Lynn have secrets?

The short answer was probably yes. Even best friends kept a few things to themselves. Like the time Camree Lynn got busted trying to sneak a beer from her parents in middle school grade. Reese had overheard her friend's ninth grade boyfriend, Jaden, complaining about her getting grounded. When Reese asked her friend about it, Camree Lynn had said she was grounded for getting a D on a math test.

So, yes, even friends lied to each other at times.

Phillip Rhodes was definitely on the list of two names.

"Do you know anyone who might have the inside track on Aiden Archer or his family?" Darren asked Buster.

"I can ask around," he said.

Darren nodded. "That might be a better approach than us showing up to ask questions."

"I'd like to see his face when he sees me, though," Reese interjected.

"Part of me agrees and the other part doesn't think it's such a good idea," Darren stated. "He might see us coming and do something…"

Reese heard what he was saying and she didn't disagree. "I still want to see his reaction."

DARREN COULDN'T ARGUE Reese's point. It was logical. However, his heart strongly disagreed. His protective instincts kicked in with every word she was saying, and he couldn't apologize for it. Explaining it didn't seem like it would do a whole lot of good, either. When Reese Hayes dug in her heels, not much could change her mind.

Worse yet, if it was him in the position instead of her, it was exactly what he would want to do. So, coming up with an argument that could persuade her to change her mind without basing it on pure emotion was difficult.

"I hear you," he began, searching for the right words, "but it could be putting you in the line of fire and I'm having a hard time thinking about doing that to someone I care about."

"We could all three go," Buster interjected. "Reese could wear something to cover her face. We still have a cowgirl hat or two around here that might work. Or a baseball cap. Something to hide her until the last minute. If I'm there, you'll have backup."

"It takes a lot to run this place," Darren pointed out. "If we're both out, the animals suffer."

"Not if we're there and back this evening," Buster

said. "In the meantime, I'll do some digging around to see if I can get a location on him."

"I'd appreciate it," Darren said. "Keep in mind the person we're looking for is dangerous and willing to destroy property. If he knows you're involved, who knows what he'll do to you."

The statement got a rise out of Buster. His eyes widened and his lips compressed into a thin line. "Let the bastard come at me."

Buster wouldn't be the kind to back down from a fight, but he needed to go in with his eyes wide open if he intended to help. Darren wanted his foreman to know the risks involved.

"Okay, then," Darren said. "As long as we're all aware of what can happen and willing to accept the risks, we can drop in on Aiden."

Reese nodded in agreement. She was about as stubborn as they came, but as beautiful, too, and his feelings toward her were clouding his viewpoint. He could admit it. Being with her again brought out feelings he didn't think existed any longer. He'd loved Hazel in his own way, but he could also admit to having closed off a large part of his heart after Reese that no one else seemed to have the key to unlock.

Which didn't mean he was saying they should go down that path with each other again. Hell, he didn't know where he stood when it came to Reese and didn't want to find out. Not now, in the middle of moving to his folks' house, fending off a would-be killer and trying to get settled for his girls so he didn't lose them to his former in-laws.

His cell buzzed, so he excused himself from the table after thanking Reese for the meal. The look of pride in her eyes wasn't helping with the attraction bit. He'd programmed in Stacie's number earlier and sent her a text.

She didn't wait for him to speak after he answered. "What happened?"

"There was a fire and—"

"Arson, you mean." Stacie wasted no time correcting him. "And I know this is because of your house guest."

"Right on both counts," he said.

The line went dead silent.

Then she said, "You have to choose between her and the girls."

He didn't like the demanding tone she used or the not-so-subtle threat. "Says who?"

"My parents, for one," Stacie returned. "And me."

"You?"

"Yes," she said with a little more fire in her tone this time.

"What do you have to do with it?" he asked.

"Darren, I don't think I've been secretive in telling you that I'm the best replacement for my sister." She'd said it like it was a job and she was the best candidate.

For this, he left the room and headed into the office. "We're not talking about a nanny job here."

"No," she replied. "We aren't. But you and I dated once. We had a spark and I think we can build something real on it."

There'd been no real attraction on his side. She was nice. They'd dated once to test the waters. "I appreciate how much you want to do what's best for the girls."

"And for us," Stacie interjected. "Hazel was always the fun one between the two of us, but I'm stable and won't aban—"

"Hazel's death was an accident," he warned. "So, I'm going to stop you right there before you say something you'll regret."

"She was reckless riding those ATVs and pushing the speed, Darren. We both know it."

"I'm about to end this call," he said. "Call back when you get your head on straight again. Okay?" He couldn't afford to anger the whole family, but this was out of line. "I'm about to hang up now if you don't say something."

"Are you sure you won't reconsider?" she asked. "Am I so horrific you can't see yourself with me. Ever?"

Again, he wasn't touching that statement.

"It's not about that," he said. "I was married to your sister, and we had these two lovely girls. It doesn't sit right with me to move on to my dead wife's sister."

"Well, putting it like that makes it sound different than I intended," she whined. "We would be two people committing to a life together. Two people who love those girls more than anything else."

"They're beyond lucky to have an aunt who is willing to sacrifice real love to make sure they're okay," he said, hoping it was enough to deflect this conversation for good. He had a sneaky suspicion it might come up again and he was already dreading the day. "And I appreciate the sacrifices you are willing to make for them."

Again, the line went quiet. Stacie didn't like what she was hearing but she wasn't rushing to respond.

"Keep me in mind," she finally said with an unusual calm. "It might be the best way for you to keep custody of the girls."

"Are you threatening me?" Darren didn't bother to hide the indignation in his tone.

"It's just my parents are, well…let's just say that I could tip the scale in your favor if we were together," she said.

Hell's bells. What was he supposed to say to that?

Rather than get worked up, he thanked her for the heads-up, and then ended the call. Were his former in-laws ready to fight? If it came down to a contest of who had more money, they would win.

The thought of losing his girls shook him to the core.

## Chapter Eighteen

Reese was finished washing the last dish when Darren joined her in the kitchen. "Buster took off to make a few phone calls and get ready to leave tonight," she said with her back still turned to him.

Darren surprised her by walking behind her and wrapping his arms around her. His breath warmed her neck as his clean spicy scent washed over her and through her. Her knees went weak, but this time for a different reason. With her back flush with his muscled chest, all kinds of tingly sensations lit up her sensitized skin.

"Who was on the phone?" she asked, wondering if the call had anything to do with the sudden display of affection. Actually, *affection* might not be the right word for it. This seemed more like he was holding on to her to gain strength.

"Stacie," he said with a tone that said the call was anything but enjoyable.

"She heard about the fire," she said.

"Yep," he admitted, but there was a whole lot more to the story based on the dread in his tone.

"Your former in-laws must be awfully riled up if Stacie was calling to check on you and maybe smooth things over," she said.

"I wouldn't say that was the exact reason for the call, but yes."

"What then?" Reese asked, her curiosity spiked.

"Let's just say, you were right about her," he admitted.

"She asked you out?"

"A little more than that," he continued.

"What's more than…oh. She asked you to marry her?" Reese asked, mortified.

"Threatened me if I didn't is more like it," he said and then laughed. It wasn't funny, but Reese laughed, too.

"What in the actual hell?" she asked when she finally stopped laughing. "Did she think you would go along with a threat?"

"I guess she believed I could be swayed with the right words," he said. Then he continued, "We did go out on a date once. But to the restaurant where her sister worked. Hazel and I met, and ended up talking. I took Stacie home and that was it."

"Stacie is out of touch if she thinks what she just asked is reasonable," Reese said with a little more emotion than intended.

"She says it's for the girls," he explained.

"Because, yes, you being forced to marry someone you don't love would be in the best interest of those babies," Reese said, incredulous. Some people had a whole lot of nerve. "Please tell me that you would never be that desperate."

Reese turned around in his arms until they were face-to-face.

"I don't feel like this when I'm around her," he said, feathering a kiss on her chin. "Or doing this." He moved lower and pressed his lips to the spot on her neck where her pulse was racing. Darren was thunder and lightning, an electrical storm of impulse.

"Good," she said. "Because I haven't felt like this with anyone in a long time."

Those words stopped him. He took in a deep breath, like he was breathing her in for the last time. And then he took a step back.

"Need any help cleaning up?" he asked, changing lanes faster than an Indy driver on a hot track.

"I'm finished now," she said, wondering what she'd said that was wrong. Then, it dawned on her that he must think she was referring to his uncle. Rather than backtrack and end up making the situation worse, she bit down on her bottom lip to keep from talking.

"You lied to me earlier," he said with a serious voice that made her dread what might come next.

"How is that?"

"You said you couldn't cook," he said, but his voice was robotic. He was forcing himself to be polite. At least she was able to read him a little bit better now. When they'd first come in contact, she'd had no idea what he could be thinking. They were easing into a rhythm and she was very clear on the moments he shut down on her. Walls came up and walls came down, just not all the way.

"I have a few tricks up my sleeve," she said. "Besides, you had the right ingredients."

"Thank Buster's wife for that," he said.

Reese wasn't sure why she should be so surprised. "Buster is married?"

"Oh, right. You wouldn't know if you hadn't kept in touch with anyone in town," Darren said, then excused himself and headed back into the office.

Reese followed.

"No, I wouldn't," she said. "And, no, I didn't." The right words didn't come to her so she just went for it. "Remember how you said young people always blame themselves for everything, even things that aren't their fault?"

He nodded as he took a seat behind the desk. She perched on the edge, making escape impossible without asking her to move. He crossed his arms over his broad chest and leaned back in the swivel chair. "Yes."

"It's because young people make foolish mistakes," she admitted. "I was one of those young people who made a terrible judgment call, but I stand behind my reasons for leaving Cider Creek and the house I grew up in. Losing you was the only mistake I made and it was huge."

He held up two fingers. "No, you made two when you started dating my uncle."

"Not that it matters now, but he was much older and manipulated me," she said. "The only dating experience I had was with you, and it spoiled me into thinking all men were honest. I never believed I deserved that again after the way I treated you. I was young and naive. And, got what I deserved when I found out he was cheating with multiple women in the office." The admission was hard. Confessions usually felt good afterward, which was the reason people finally owned up to something. Admitting she'd been played for a fool was embarrassing. "I thought I was mature enough to handle anything when I left Cider Creek. But I was dead wrong. I sank into a hole because I missed you so much I could barely breathe. And then your uncle started showing up at my house, bringing food. He said I didn't look like I was eating, and he wanted to make sure his star intern was doing okay with the big move."

Darren sat there, stone-faced. She had no idea if she was getting through or just making a bigger fool of herself, but she had no plans to stop now that she'd gotten the ball rolling.

"Do I regret leaving home?" she asked. "The answer is no. Do I regret the way I left you? One hundred percent, yes. Would I change everything if I could go back and do it all over again?" She nodded even though he stared down at the wood flooring. "I'm sorry for the way I treated you and I have no right to ask anything of you, but—"

He looked up, catching her gaze and stopping her in midsentence. "We're already friends, Reese. You don't have to ask."

A tear escaped, streaking down her cheek.

"With the twins and running the ranch, I can't say that leaves a whole lot of time left over for anything else," he said. "But we started out as friends and I'd like it very much if we could get back to that."

"Same for me," she said. *Grateful* didn't begin to describe the way she felt at the possibility he wouldn't hate her for the rest of her life. The notion they might actually be friends, even if it was distant, made her feel like anything was possible.

She was also realizing how quickly she'd adjusted to being away from her cell. Normally, it was like an additional appendage and she got heart palpitations when she couldn't find it for even a couple of minutes. Then, there were those times she searched for it while it was still in her hand. Those were doozies. But, mostly, she was glued to the small screen.

Being around Darren almost had her wishing she could lose her phone more often. This was probably the most she'd spoken to one person without constant pings from her phone. She babysat a lot of her clients and the term *babysat* was appropriate. They could be demanding and throw temper tantrums when they didn't get their way.

Despite someone being intent on erasing her permanently, she was surprisingly calm when she was close to Darren. It was a foreign feeling now.

DARREN DIDN'T HAVE the heart to kick Reese in the teeth when she was baring her soul. He was being honest, too. He didn't have a whole lot of time for friends, but this ordeal had brought them back together and he still cared whether or not she lived or died. He would like to hear from her every once in a while, even if it was from afar. The girls wouldn't be little forever and he needed to remember that fact, because he should also think about having a small life for himself. Something separate that wouldn't make them miss him like they already would their mother. Like he'd told Stacie, maybe it was time to think about dating again. The thought of having someone to talk to at the end of the day, even if it was just a phone call to check in with each other, was becoming more and more appealing.

Of course, that all had to be put on hold now that Stacie had lost her mind and his former in-laws might be suing him for custody.

"So as your friend, I'd like you to talk to me about what's going on right now," Reese said, interrupting his heavy thoughts.

"I was just thinking about custody and doing what's best for the girls," he said. "A long court battle where I'm in a fight with their grandparents will only push us further apart. We'd been working together okay. Or at least I thought we had. It's hard to believe they're bringing up the possibility of fighting me for custody again. I thought I'd proved myself more than capable of bringing these girls up alone in the last year."

"They are probably still grieving, which doesn't excuse their behavior," she said.

"I gave them plenty of latitude on that one," he said. "But at some point, I have to remind them that I was married to their daughter."

"You must have missed her something awful,"

Reese said with the kind of compassion that could heal an open sore in two seconds flat.

"I still do," he admitted. "When the girls do something new, like the first time Ivy walked. She's the youngest but is never to be outdone by her older by two minutes sister. Ivy got this big grin on her face and then just threw herself toward me. My heart nearly exploded at seeing my girl take her first steps, but then the sadness hit because her mother should be here to witness it, too."

"Kids shouldn't have to grow up without a parent," Reese agreed as a mix of emotions passed behind her eyes that she immediately tried to cover.

"I'm a jerk," he said. "I'm sorry. You grew up without your father because—"

"You don't have to apologize," she interrupted. "Besides, we were talking about your family, not mine."

He shook his head. Seeing the pain in her eyes made him wonder if he would see that same look in his own daughters one day.

"It's okay," she said. "Really, it is."

"Talk to me, Reese."

"No. It's just that my dad obviously missed a lot of my childhood...*most* of my childhood. I was so little when he died that I have no memories of him," she said. "We never talked about him when I was growing up, but I'm starting to realize that might have been Duncan's fault, too. All I want to say is that you should keep pictures of their mother up and tell them stories about her when they're older. They'll want to hear them but might be afraid to ask. Kids have a way of picking up on emotions, and talking about her makes you sad, so..."

"That's good advice, Reese." He locked gazes for a second longer than was good for his heart. "I'll keep that in mind."

"Good," she said. "That will keep her memory alive and they need that because it's the only way they'll know how much she loved them and what kind of person she was."

He nodded. "I bet your mother would love to talk to you about your dad."

"We don't ask because we think it'll be painful for her to talk about," she said.

"It's not," he said. "In fact, widowers want their children to know about your other parent. But I can see how life happens and the subject just doesn't come up after a while. Years pass and we move on with our lives, and it's easy not to go back and talk about it."

"Makes sense," she admitted. "But I can also see that I've been way too hard on my own mother. She deserves a break. And a hug, as far as I'm concerned. After talking to you, I'm starting to see how hard the job is."

"Marla is a good person," he said. "She definitely deserves a hug."

"She always liked you," Reese said. "I was half afraid she would never want to hear from me again after the way I treated you. It's probably the reason I took so long to get into contact with her along with many others. Plus, I believed she would try to talk me into coming back home, which she did."

"You've done good for yourself, Reese." He meant

that. "You should be proud of the work you've accomplished."

She shook her head.

"I'm in an endless loop of taking care of people who are only bothered right now because they can't reach me," she corrected. "It's not like ranching communities, where people take care of each other."

"Careful there," he teased, trying to lighten the mood. "I'll start thinking you miss Hayes Cattle."

She looked him straight in the eye. "You know, I never thought I'd hear those words come out of my own mouth. I'm busy in Dallas and I do okay. But, at the end of the day, no one there is looking out for me or after me right now. The only people calling me want me to do something for them. And I convinced myself that was a real life, a better life."

"And now?"

"Being here at your parents' place—*your* place now—I feel like I'm at home for the first time in a long time," she said. "But then, that might just be because you're here. I felt it at your house before, too."

"Do you mean that?" he asked.

"I sure do," she said. "I'm not saying that I want to give up my business." She shook her head like she could shake off the thought. "I don't know what it means for my future but being away from it for the first time in…ever…has me thinking that maybe I want to make some changes in my life."

Did those changes involve him? Better yet, did he want them to?

## Chapter Nineteen

The revelations hit Reese square in the chest, but she couldn't do anything about them until the person trying to kill her was caught. She'd showered and eaten. They had a big night ahead of them. If she stayed inside this office any longer with Darren looking at her like he was, she might just say something she would regret later.

"I should probably get some rest before we head out this evening," she said to him, needing an excuse to step away.

"Yeah," he said, and his voice was heavy with emotion. "That's probably a good idea."

"Mind if I rest next door and keep these open?" She motioned toward the door as she stood up.

"Be my guest," he said, then went back to studying the screen in his hand.

Reese walked to the master bedroom, then curled up on top of the covers. Darren had moved on to the computer keyboard and there was something reassuring about the *click-click-click* of the keyboard. There was a rhythm to his movements. Knowing he was right next door helped her doze in and out of sleep over the next few hours, then it was time to get up. She freshened up in the bathroom and headed down the hall toward the office.

She stopped at the door, took one look at Darren while he was deep in thought and a picture was imprinted on her thoughts. It was her, Darren and the girls living together in this home as a family. The tree was up, the girls were a couple of years older and Reese was resting a hand on her baby bump.

Did she want those things? Or was she having a career crisis? Was she burned out from working for a decade without a real vacation? She'd taken her phone with her on every trip, every weekend.

Reese flexed and released her fingers, realizing for maybe the first time how good it felt not to have them wrapped around a phone.

She was taking deeper breaths now, too, realizing life was short and she wanted to breathe fresh air again. If she moved home, she could probably run her business from here and only need to make trips to Dallas a few days every month to handle things in person. She could also hire a manager to help run her small service company.

"Hey."

Darren's voice pulled her from her deep thoughts. She looked up at him only to realize he was studying her.

"What are you thinking about?" he asked.

He probably didn't want to know all of it, especially the fantasy about him and the girls, so she said,

"Changes that need to happen in my life if we're able to—"

"Not if," he interrupted. "When."

She stared at him, loving that he believed everything would work out great. Her reality didn't always go the way she'd planned. Still, his heart was in the right place, and she didn't have it in her to disagree. "Okay, *when* we're able to lock this bastard or bastards away."

Darren clicked off the computer he'd been working on and led the way into the kitchen. "Coffee?"

"I'd love some," she said, "but only if you let me help."

The two worked together to put on a fresh pot. She rinsed out their mugs from earlier.

"It'll be dark soon," she said. "When did Buster say he was coming back?"

Darren glanced at the clock on the wall. "We have about half an hour."

She nodded.

"I have bad news about Phillip Rhodes," he said.

"Oh yeah? What's that?"

"He just finished chemo recently," Darren said. "I was able to track down one of his family members. The guy is a jerk for what he did to you. Apparently, he found religion five years ago and has been working the same job ever since. His mother said that he had to move in with her six months ago so she could care for him during treatment."

"I hope he did get his life together," she said. It didn't change what he'd done to her, but she didn't have it in her heart to wish cancer on anyone. "But it doesn't sound like he would be strong enough to force someone to go with him."

Darren took a sip of coffee. "No. He's off the list. Which leaves Aiden Archer. He's more of a mystery."

"Which doesn't mean he's guilty," she pointed out, frustrated they didn't have a few more names to go on. It would be fine if Aiden was the one, but what if he wasn't? Narrowing down the suspect list to one name was hard.

"I know," he said. "We'll find this guy. I promise."

It wasn't a guarantee that anyone could make right now, but she appreciated him for trying to offer some reassurance.

"I heard you typing," she said, changing the subject.

"Ranch work is a whole lot of paperwork," he said with a look that said he saw what she was doing.

"Do you still love it?" she asked.

"I love being here on the land," he said. "You know how much I love the animals. The paperwork? That's not my favorite part."

"You never were one for doing homework," she quipped. "Despite the fact you tested better than me."

"It was busywork for people who couldn't understand the material," he insisted with a small quirk of a smile.

"Not everyone is a genius, like you," she said.

"Some genius," he countered. "I let the one person I truly loved get away without even trying to find you. How smart was I?"

The look on his face said his comment surprised

him as much as it did her. An awkward moment passed before Reese took another sip of coffee and then walked over to the kitchen sink.

"This land always was beautiful," she said. "I loved coming here."

"Sometimes, I get so busy with life that I forget to stop and appreciate everything I do have," he said. "Having this place makes me feel connected to something bigger than myself."

"I can see that," she said. "My business might be successful and I like what I do most of the time, but there's no legacy. It doesn't tie into anything bigger in the way Hayes Cattle does."

"It's understandable how you might think that way, but you've built something from scratch," he said. "There is a whole lot to be proud of in that."

"Thank you, Darren." Those words, coming from him, meant more than she could say.

FORTY-FIVE MINUTES TICKED BY. Waiting was the absolute worst. If Darren paced anymore, he'd wear a hole in the carpet, metaphorically speaking, since the floors were wood.

Buster came through the back door at 6:30 p.m. "The Archer family sticks to themselves. No one knows all that much about them other than the fact they run the bee farm on the outskirts of Cider Creek."

"I don't remember much about Aiden from school, but I believe he would have been two grades ahead of us," Darren said as Reese listened intently.

"You probably don't know him because he dropped

out of school in the ninth grade," Buster said. "I asked around and Mrs. Carmen said she was one of his teachers. Said he was a quiet boy who was unapproachable. He used to get bullied because he didn't talk much, and she remembered feeling sorry for him because of it. It's the reason he stuck out in her mind. His parents pulled him to homeschool him, saying they needed the extra help around the farm."

"The guy sounds like he could fit the description of a would-be serial killer," Reese finally said.

"It definitely doesn't rule him out," Buster admitted.

"I hate to say this, but living on a remote bee farm would give him a lot of places to bury bodies," Darren pointed out. "Aiden would know the land like the back of his hand and could have cameras set up, hidden."

"Which would also make it hard for us to confront him," Reese said. "We have no idea if he's home."

Buster lifted his index finger. "The place takes deliveries. Aiden is rarely, if ever, seen, according to several of the folks I spoke to but that doesn't mean he doesn't slip out at night and disappear for a couple of days to go somewhere. He's never seen in town, though."

"How would he know the girls if he doesn't leave the property?" Reese asked.

"Good question," Darren said. "Since the cases are stretched far apart, he might study each one and take his time with them."

Could it mean Tandra was still alive? Could they get to her in time?

"I'm ready when you are," Buster said.

Darren nodded before retrieving a baseball cap for Reese. Even with the disguise, Darren would know it was her from a mile away. If Aiden was targeting her, he would, too. So, basically, Darren had the drive over to convince her to stay inside the vehicle.

"Whoever is responsible for this also lit my home on fire," Darren said. "If we come driving up in my SUV, it'll alert Aiden and/or whoever else might be involved."

"Then, we'll take my pickup," Buster said. "It has a bench seat in front, plenty big enough to fit all three of us."

Reese put on the cap, lowering the rim to hide as much of her face as possible. Then, Darren waited for her to lead the way outside. It dawned on him that he might need a weapon of his own. His mother would never allow loaded guns inside the house and he respected her wishes to this day even though she wasn't there. It was one of many small ways that he kept her memory alive at the farmhouse.

It was already dark outside when Darren went to the locked shed at the back of the house. Clouds rolled across a blue velvet sky. He unlocked it and then retrieved the Colt .45 he kept there for shooting coyotes. It was the quickest way to get rid of the menace. There were wild boars on the property, too, and they were nasty creatures. Mean, too.

The drive over was quiet. The gate to the bee farm was closed. Was it locked?

Buster exited the vehicle and opened the metal gate.

The porch light was on at the ranch-style home. They were expected, so someone must have heard them driving up. And the prickly hair feeling on the back of Darren's neck was on high alert. He felt like they were being watched.

"You feel that?" he asked Reese and Buster. It didn't need explaining, not with how quiet they were. The cab was eerily silent.

"Yep," Buster finally said.

"I do, too," Reese agreed.

He pulled up beside the house and cut the engine. "Since they appear to know we're here, I say we all three go inside. It'll be safer if we all stick together."

"I was just about to suggest the same thing," Darren stated as he opened the passenger door and exited the truck. He helped Reese out next as Buster came around from the driver's side.

There was safety in numbers. He and Buster flanked Reese, ignoring the ominous feeling. This place gave him the creeps.

As they stepped onto the porch, the front door cracked open.

"Mrs. Archer, I'm Buster Wren." He stretched out a hand as a gray pit bull let out a low, throaty growl from her side.

"He's not friendly," Mrs. Archer said, referring to the dog.

Out in these parts with the house tucked behind a metal gate, Darren wondered what the need for an angry pit bull might be. He understood needing protection for cattle, but these were beekeepers not ranchers.

"I'm Darren Pierce," he said when her gaze shifted to him.

"And my name is Ree—"

"You're a Hayes," Mrs. Archer said in a disgusted tone. "I know who you are."

That tone sent a cold chill racing up Darren's back.

"We'd like to talk to you and your husband, if possible," Darren said. There was no way to get a peek inside the place with how little the door was cracked. All the brothers could be back there standing behind the door for all Darren knew.

Another thing occurred to him. The family had no storefront. They sold to businesses. And businesses needed deliveries. Darren would bet money Aiden and his brothers did the driving. There was a bigger question looming. Was this a family affair?

## Chapter Twenty

Reese took a step back and to her right. Darren seemed to understand what she was doing when he brought his shoulder forward and tucked her behind him.

"What can I help you with?" Mrs. Archer said. The older woman looked hard. A couple of her teeth were missing, and her sun-worn skin was wrinkled, especially around the eyes. Hers were an intense shade of green, piercing and distrustful. Her mouth was bracketed by deep grooves. This was not a kind face. This was not the face of a good person. This was the face of someone hardened by life.

Mrs. Archer's strawberry-blond hair was in a messy pile on top of her head. Her clothing was a flannel dress, which oddly suited her. She kept her right arm hidden behind the door. Reese would bet money the woman was gripping a shotgun.

"Is your husband home?" Buster continued. Being the eldest of the group, he would command the most respect. His voice was calm but stern.

"I never said he wasn't," Mrs. Archer replied. Yeah, her responses were firing off warning shots left and right. A part of Reese wanted to head back into the truck, get inside and keep driving until she could no longer be tracked.

One thought kept her from turning around. Was Tandra still alive?

The feeling of pure evil was thick despite the cool breeze that said winter was gaining ground.

"Could we speak to him?" Buster continued, unfazed, but he had to be feeling the same thing as Reese. She could tell by Darren's tense muscles that he did.

"I'll see if I can find him," she said after a long pause. "Stay right here or Tyson will get nervous."

The door closed. While they waited, she figured it might be a good time to check out the place a little.

The porch was lit up. Seeing much past a small area was next to impossible since there were no other lights on the property. At least, no others that were on. Insects chirped, giving Reese a bad case of the willies. She might have been born in ranching country, but she never liked the thought of insects crawling on or around her. Field mice used to get inside the house occasionally and those really freaked her out. So, yes, she was on high alert.

Not to mention the possibility of coming face-to-face with a man who wanted to kill her.

Reese involuntarily shivered.

The door swung open wide. A tall man in suspenders she assumed to be Mr. Archer filled the space.

"What the hell do you want?" he grunted. "You have about ten seconds to tell me what you're doing on my property before I tell you to leave."

The door opened wide enough to give a glimpse of a shotgun. Reese had no doubts the man was prepared to use it.

Buster's hands came up in the surrender position. "Hold on there, Mr. Archer. We didn't come to get into a confrontation."

Reese started to back away slowly from the door.

"Then, why have you come?" Mr. Archer continued. "Because I don't take kindly to strangers meddling in my business or folks intent on trespassing on my land."

The reaction to their visit was over-the-top. Fear raced through Reese as she cleared the porch. She wouldn't put it past the family to make up a story about the three of them after shooting them. Then again, if Tandra was here, would they want to risk being found out?

The adrenaline jolt Reese was experiencing was the equivalent of a double shot of espresso. Her heart thundered inside her rib cage as her gaze scanned every place the light touched.

"We'll just be leaving now," Buster said as he hopped down from the porch.

The dog could be unleashed on them. They were on Archer land. Texas would back the land owners if they were mauled, especially if the Archers claimed the trio were trespassing.

Reese was torn between getting the heck out of Dodge and probing to find out if Tandra was here.

"Get inside the pickup as fast as you can," Darren said out of the side of his mouth. He spoke barely loud enough for her to hear.

She didn't wait for a second invitation. Reese turned and made a beeline for the truck, not stopping to look up until she was safely inside.

"Oops," Mr. Archer said before making a weak attempt to call his dog back.

Reese turned in time to see the dog clearing the porch in one jump. Darren hurried inside the truck and Buster followed a few seconds later.

"Did that bastard just sic his dog on us?" she asked, incredulous.

"Are those the actions of an innocent man?" Buster growled. He started the engine and backed down the lane.

On the side of the gravel lane, the headlights showed two men with weapons hiding in the shadows. They looked like the Archer boys.

"Do you see those bastards?" Reese asked, motioning toward the left. They were about twenty feet apart on the same side of the road.

"Sure do," Darren stated, pulling out a weapon and keeping it behind the dashboard, out of view. He wasn't taking any chances but didn't want to instigate trouble, either. She appreciated his caution because this place seemed like a teapot on a burning hot stove ready to boil over any second. The tension in the air was thick.

"We can't leave," Reese said without a whole lot of conviction. They *had* to leave but they couldn't abandon Tandra if she was here.

"I know," Darren said quietly. "We just need a better plan to figure out if she's here."

Darren issued a sharp sigh. "If Tandra is alive, she might not be for long now that we showed up, poking around."

"Did we just issue a death sentence to a fifteen-year-old girl if she's not already dead?" Reese asked, horrified.

Darren let out a sharp sigh. He knew she was right. Buster didn't offer a differing opinion, either.

"It's impossible to know for certain," Darren finally said as they left property. "Staying here will get us killed and we are of no help to Tandra if we're silenced."

He made a good point, and it was along the lines of what she was thinking, too. They were stuck between a rock and a hard place.

"How about you guys drop me, and I'll circle back?" Buster said.

"With Tyson running around?" Reese asked. "You can't do that."

"Plus, the others might be walking the property for a while to make sure we didn't get any bright ideas," Darren said.

The sheriff believing them would make this a whole lot easier. Going back on the property without permission was trespassing, and it was legal to shoot them on sight.

"What can we do?" she asked in frustration.

"We'll think of something," Darren reassured her. He was picking up his girls tomorrow at noon. All investigating needed to stop for him at that point.

"We go back," Buster said. "Let's give it a couple of hours and then circle back."

As far as ideas went, it sounded like suicide. What else did they have?

DARREN WAS ABOUT to suggest the same thing as Buster, except that he was trying to figure out a way to keep Reese out of it. She would protest, and he didn't have a good argument as to why she couldn't go with them other than the same keeping-her-safe excuse that she'd rejected before. He knew her, and him asking her not to go while he risked his own life wasn't an option, either. She could be stubborn that way.

Buster drove a couple miles down the farm road before cutting the lights and pulling off the road. "Those folks are guilty as sin of something."

"Yep, they are," Darren agreed.

"Murder is a serious accusation," Buster continued.

"Kidnapping and murder," Reese added. "If this is true, they're preying on teenagers."

"Deliveries across the state sure make a good excuse to be in various places," Darren added.

"Not to mention, they use trucks, which would make it easy to hide someone," Reese added.

"It's all circumstantial," Buster said. "We don't have any proof. Just a theory."

"A good one at that," Reese stated.

"Not enough for the law to step in," Buster said. "Like we already said, the best they could do would be to drop by and ask questions. The Archers don't have to allow them inside even if they have a kid strapped to the couch. The law wouldn't be any wiser. Without a search warrant, they can't walk through the door or make demands."

"So we go back," Darren said. "This could be like searching for a needle in a haystack."

"Not to mention these people are beekeepers," Buster added. "They'll have storage buildings for their honey and others for equipment. There's no telling where they would stash a fifteen-year-old."

"Assuming we're right in the first place and she is actually here," Reese added.

"And still alive," Darren pointed out. The odds weren't great they would be able to make a hill-of-beans difference. And yet, if this was one of his girls, he would hope folks would move heaven and earth to find out before walking away.

"What if we're off base?" Buster asked. "Just playing devil's advocate here."

"Then, we know for sure the Archers are innocent," Darren said. "We keep looking for Tandra while trying to figure out who is trying to kill Reese." Those last words tasted bitter in his mouth. "Because whoever is behind this is intent on making sure she doesn't see her next birthday."

"And they don't mind taking down anyone who is helping me," Reese added. "Now that the two of you have shown your faces, neither one is safe."

Darren nodded. He was well aware of the danger, considering his house had been torched. Those smug bastards weren't getting away with it, either. "With the whole family involved, they could easily cover each other's tracks."

"Seems like everyone has a computer, laptop or smartphone these days," Reese said. "Any one of them could be responsible for finding the next target and grooming them."

"If that's true, the family isn't just criminal, they're..." Darren stopped himself right there. His emotions were running high, and he didn't need to finish his sentence. The thought this could happen to one of his girls at some point in their lives was enough to make him crack a tooth from clenching his teeth so hard.

"We'll figure something out," Reese insisted. "I wish we had a reason to be on property. That would make this so much easier."

"Or an invitation," Buster quipped.

"I wonder if there are any other dogs like Tyson on property?" Reese asked.

"I'm guessing just the one since we haven't heard barking, and it seems like they keep him at the house," Buster mused. "We would have heard others mouthing off once Tyson got riled up."

There was a small miracle. Still, if they made the pit bull angry and got anywhere near his mouth, the bite from his jaw would apply something like three hundred pounds of pressure. The jaw would lock, too, so there was no opening it again or wriggling out. Plus, this one looked trained to defend. Not good.

"So, with the Archers, we're dealing with at least

two young men, a mother, a father and an aggressive dog," Reese recapped.

"I wouldn't underestimate any one of those," Darren added. "To complicate matters, we're going on gut instinct these folks have done something illegal. They might just be nasty folks who keep to themselves. Jerks but not criminals."

"This family strikes me as pure evil," Reese said.

"We can all agree there," Buster interjected.

"We know that we want to circle back and explore the property," Darren said. "But doing it safely is the issue."

"Hell, I forgot all about that drone thing I got for Christmas last year," Buster said. "My wife thought it would be a good way to check on the cattle near Dangling Creek. You know how one ends up there stuck in the mud every spring."

"I do," Darren said, liking the sound of this idea. "I'm guessing it has some kind of light for a night feature."

Buster nodded. "We can go back and study the property using those internet maps."

"That would help us figure out where we could best enter," Darren agreed, starting to gain a little more momentum with the idea.

"It could also save one of us from getting shot," Reese added.

"And give us a bird's-eye view of who might be patrolling around," Darren said.

"I would bet money the family will be setting up patrol at least over the next couple of hours," Buster said.

"A couple of hours gives us enough time to go home, collect the drone and figure out the landscape," Darren said. "The actual ranch land will be blurred online, but we'll get a sense of the periphery."

A plan was taking shape. It was still risky, but doable with minimal collateral damage, he hoped. The thought of something bad happening to Buster or Reese sat hard on his chest. He was a single father. His girls needed him. He needed to come home in one piece.

Would voluntarily stepping into a life-threatening situation be enough for him to lose custody if his in-laws had a good lawyer?

He couldn't ignore the possibility. Or the developing feelings he had for Reese. They went beyond ensuring her well-being. He could be honest with himself about it. The thought she might not make it off the Archer property alive nearly gutted him. As much as he was ready to make sure justice was served, the idea of going back to his old routine—a routine that didn't involve Reese—sat heavy, too.

But could he open his heart to her a second time?

## *Chapter Twenty-One*

The drive back to the farmhouse was spent in quiet contemplation. Reese leaned her head on Darren's shoulder and closed her eyes for most of the ride.

Buster pulled up beside the farmhouse.

"I'll grab the drone and meet you at the house," he said, then headed toward the barn and bunkhouse, where he and his wife lived.

Reese followed Darren inside and straight to the laptop on the counter. She claimed one of the bar stools and Darren took the open one next to her. He turned on the computer and then pulled up the map. As expected, the actual property was a blur. However, since it butted up against roads, they could move that way to get a sense of the periphery.

"It would be nice if we could bring this with us," she said.

"I could create a hot spot with my cell…"

He shook his head.

"Not sure about this throwaway," he said. Then he got up and retrieved a pad of paper and pen from the office. "Then again, nothing like going about this the old-fashioned way."

Darren drew a rough map of the Archer Bee Farm.

"We should probably be ready to call the law at any moment while we're there," Reese pointed out.

"Do you want to be in charge of that?" he asked.

She nodded.

"Good," he said. "When we get there, I'll hand over the phone."

"I imagine Buster will man the drone," she said.

"I have some night-vision goggles that we can bring," Darren added. "They'll come in handy if we need to go on property."

"How long does a drone battery last?" she asked.

Darren's fingers danced across the keyboard after he pulled up a search engine. "Let's see. Not long. Maybe half an hour."

"Which is why we need a solid lay of the land before we send it in," she said.

"Says here they can fly anywhere from forty to sixty miles per hour," he stated.

"That should help cover a lot of ground."

Darren leaned back. "It's the safest way to get on the property and the most efficient. But I'm thinking that any evidence we gather won't be able to be used in a court of law."

"Which could mean those bastards might walk away," she said.

"If we find Tandra and she can testify." He paused for a few seconds, stopping before saying *if* she can testify, because he hoped she wasn't dead. "Then we're okay."

"We had a question for the family and stopped by to ask," she proposed.

"But if we don't find anything, or something truly bad happens, all three of us can be arrested, sued or both," Darren said. Which meant he was risking more than his livelihood.

Darren stood to lose everything. They needed to find something or leave without getting caught.

Before she could tell him that he didn't have to do this, he said, "I'm all in, Reese."

"I wouldn't be able to live with myself if anything happened to you and those girls were orphans or, heaven forbid both scenarios, you were sued and couldn't provide for them any longer," she said as a tear escaped.

"I love that you are always putting my girls first, but I am, too," he said. "How could I call myself a father or live with myself if Tandra is alive in there and we could save her? I understand the risk I'm taking, and I didn't commit to this lightly. As much as I'm doing this to keep you safe, my girls are always at the forefront of my thoughts, and I wouldn't be able to look them in the eyes if I let someone else's daughter die when I could have saved her. Plus, this might help resolve the other cases, as well."

"You're an amazing father, Darren. And an even better human being," Reese said. She'd known it back in high school, and she'd been an idiot for letting him go. At least he'd agreed to be friends, moving forward. She wanted very much to be in his life.

Buster knocked, then unlocked the back door and walked into the kitchen. "The drone is in the pickup. We can head out whenever you two are ready." He took a step inside and waited by the door.

Darren stood up. He picked up the notepad and showed the rudimentary map to Buster, who gave a nod of appreciation.

"I think we should come from the opposite side to confuse them," Darren said, pointing to the east side of the property.

"Good idea," Buster said. "I was just thinking along those same lines. We definitely don't want to go in the way we came earlier. They'll be expecting that."

"My thinking exactly," Darren said. "Plus, there's a cluster of small buildings tucked over here, away from the main house."

They headed out the back door, making sure the place was secure before making their way to the pickup parked beside the farmhouse.

Reese looked at the house as Buster backed up and was overcome with a strange sensation. Was this the last time she would see the place that had been a second home to her? She cleared her throat, unable and unwilling to allow herself to believe all three of them wouldn't make it back alive. Besides, she was working herself up for the worst-case scenario. The whole thing might end up a bust. The drone could reveal no wrongdoing and they could end up turning around to come back home.

Home? Interesting word choice.

Ready or not, it was go time.

DARREN STUDIED HIS homemade map like his life de-
pended on it, and was using the flashlight app on his
throwaway cell phone on dim. He'd mapped out the
house, the tree line on the west side of the driveway.
He'd made two dots where the pair of boys had been
standing. They'd been protecting their home while
taking cover. Had they believed things might go south
during the visit? Were they meant to be a warning?

The fact they'd decided to stand where they could
be seen meant they were sending a message. They
meant business. Darren made no mistake about it. If
what they believed was true, members of this family would be locked away for a very long time, if not
the rest of their lives. Even if their mother wasn't
involved, she would go down as an accomplice. He
didn't need to be in law enforcement to know these
folks had nothing to lose, which made them even more
dangerous.

Of course, if they were innocent...

Darren stopped himself right there. The place had
the security of a meth lab, and he seriously doubted
the Archer family was running drugs out of there. Although, he couldn't be one-hundred-percent certain
about that, either. Uncertainty was the worst.

Archer Bee Farm was a family operation, so were
there cousins, uncles or nieces who were involved
with the business?

More questions looped through his thoughts as

Buster passed by the entrance to the farm. He circled around to the west side of the property, driving along a dirt road. A few miles into the turn, he pulled to the side and parked.

The area was surrounded by trees and scrub brush. The pathway was well-worn, which meant vehicles used this stretch a fair amount since it wasn't gravel or pavement. That might be a good sign they weren't totally off base with the theory.

"Since this thing has a light on it, I'll have to maneuver it through the trees instead of over them," Busted began as he exited the driver's side. He retrieved the drone from the back as Darren slipped out the passenger side before helping Reese out.

That was the hope.

Darren took in a deep breath before releasing it slowly.

"Before we move ahead, I just want to thank both of you for everything you're doing," Reese whispered. "I do realize this isn't just for me, but that doesn't take anything away from my gratitude."

"You'd do the same," Buster said, waving her off.

Darren reached for her hand, and then squeezed for reassurance.

Buster motioned toward the fence line. "I'll head down this way with the drone. Do you want to follow or stay by the pickup?"

"We should keep watch here until you find something," Darren said. "In fact, you might want to hand over the keys in case we need to get away fast."

Buster reached into his front pocket and then tossed

them over. This pickup was old enough to need an actual key. "I'll give you a shout if I find anything."

"Got it," Darren said. "Good luck."

If Tandra was being held here, he hoped they were in time. It was late at this point, long past midnight. They'd visited hours ago and might have caused the Archers to panic. Would they lie low? Would they ramp up? Would they kill her and dispose of the body? Once again, the property was large. But there were only a few areas that might be good for dumping a body. They wouldn't do it near water, so as not to contaminate it as the body decomposed.

Darren stopped himself from going down too morbid a road. Waiting for Buster to return was the pits.

Thankfully, they didn't have to wait too much longer. Darren came running, waving his arms in the air.

Darren immediately jumped into the pickup, as did Reese, and then cranked the engine. Buster hopped into the back and rolled, keeping a low profile.

"Stay low," Darren said to Reese as he backed down the drive without headlights. He didn't plan to stick around long enough to find out what had spooked Buster. They could regroup when it was safe.

Reese ducked down in the seat and he made himself as small as possible. Not an easy feat for someone his size and stature. In fact, he was the biggest target in the vehicle.

Half-expecting gunfire to break out and half-expecting someone to jump out from behind a tree, he was surprised when nothing happened for a couple of miles until he made it onto the farm road.

Buster knocked on the glass, so Darren took that as a sign to stop. He joined them inside the cab.

"What did you get?" Darren asked.

"They were patrolling on that side," Buster said. "I had to get out of there."

"On foot?" Darren asked.

"They must have anticipated us, or this is their normal routine," Buster said. "One of them heard the drone but didn't know what it was."

"No one would be out walking around this time of night unless they were concerned we would come back and find something," Reese interjected.

Darren nodded. "We can go back to the other side to the entrance area and watch."

"It's the best we can do for now," Buster said. "I didn't see any buildings on this side of the property, anyway."

"Do you know how many of them were out there?" Darren asked.

"I'm pretty sure it was the pair from earlier," Buster said.

"Seems like they would send someone else to cover this side if they had them," Reese pointed out. She wasn't wrong. Darren made the same assumption.

"At least we can reasonably assume we aren't dealing with a small army here," Buster said.

It was a small miracle. One he'd take. The family consisted of three boys, who would now be grown men. Two had been on patrol. Where was the third one?

"At this point, we know there are four people in the house, possibly involved," Buster said. "I have enough battery left on the drone to investigate the area around the house."

"You don't think they would keep her in the main house, do you?" Reese asked, sounding mortified.

Buster shrugged his shoulders as Darren turned on the fog lights and kept driving. No one was out on the road this time of night. This area could be described as one that rolled the streets up by 8:00 p.m. Not much happened past sunset. Of course, folks would be up in a few hours. Rising at four o'clock in the morning was normal rancher hours.

Darren drove around to the entrance of Archer Bee Farm, and then continued twenty yards past it. He pulled over and turned off the engine. He retrieved the notepad, then handed it over to Buster. "Mark the spot where you saw the guys on patrol."

Buster did.

"I wish we had our bearings," Darren said. "My map could be off."

"We aren't getting anywhere," Reese said.

Giving up when they were this close to figuring out the truth wasn't something Darren wanted to consider. And yet, Reese had a point. They weren't getting any closer to finding Tandra and it was too risky to barge onto the farm at this hour.

But what choice did they have?

## Chapter Twenty-Two

Reese twisted her fingers together, tying them in a knot. "We have to go in."

"I know," Darren said and then Buster agreed.

"Good," she said.

"It's not ideal," Darren continued. "But we can get a cursory look through the drone and possibly get enough intel to know how to target our search."

"Otherwise, this is an almost impossible find," Reese agreed.

"Let's do this again," Buster said. "It's getting late. Or early, depending on your point of view."

All three exited the pickup. This time, Reese took the keys and they decided to stick together. After backtracking toward the entrance, they found a hole in the fence and slipped through.

"The closer we get to possibilities, the longer life we get out of the battery," Buster pointed out as they moved through scrub brush and trees. They stayed close to the gravel drive as they moved, making as little noise as possible.

The occasional rustling of leaves nearly stopped Reese's heart. She reminded herself to breathe.

On foot, they made it close to the family residence, sticking to the tree line. The house was pitch-black now and there was no sign of movement inside or around it. She'd been praying they hadn't tripped a silent alarm, but the men patrolling and the dog seemed to be the two main sources of security.

Once safely past the house, Buster sent the drone out. He kept it low to the ground until he found a clearing. He located the hives about a quarter of a mile from the house.

"Looks like the hives are spaced around five hundred feet apart," Buster informed them after studying the screen on the control panel. "There has to be a building where they keep supplies and jar the honey. Right?"

"I would think so," Darren concluded.

"Might be a good place to hold someone against their will," Buster said.

"Is it the obvious choice, though?" Reese asked. "The Archer family doesn't strike me as the most brilliant people in the world based on the parents, but that doesn't mean they aren't criminally smart."

"What's your idea?" Darren asked in a voice barely above a whisper.

"I don't know," she admitted. "I'm just thinking out loud."

Her eyes had adjusted to the dark enough to see Darren nod. It was getting cold outside. She shoved her hands inside her pockets to keep them warm. What were they missing?

And then it dawned on her.

"What about the trucks?" she asked.

"It would make for an easy escape if she was already loaded up," Darren said.

"I got a building," Buster whispered. "What do you think about splitting up again?"

"It's risky, but we'll cover more ground that way," Darren said.

Reese agreed, so she didn't speak up. There was no denying the risks or the fact they would be more productive this way. Time was of the essence and their window of opportunity was quickly closing. So, yeah, they needed to do whatever it took.

Buster gave each one a quick hug before heading toward the building. She and Darren circled back to the trucks that were lined up near the main house. There were three trucks parked off to the side of the home. The house was a side yard away from the small gravel lot, so roughly half a football field if she had to guess.

They couldn't afford to make noise and awaken the scary dog in the house. Darren tucked her behind him as they neared the first truck. It was a small commercial delivery vehicle with one of those rolling metal doors in the back. A twist of a handle revealed it wasn't locked.

Slowly, methodically, Darren raised the door. He palmed his cell and tapped the flashlight feature. There were bucket shelves lining the sides, easy for tucking in jars of honey for transport. The vehicle was empty. They moved to truck number two. It was empty as well. Truck number three was no different.

So much for the truck idea.

Darren turned around and sat down on the bumper of truck number three. "Something is off." He shook his head. "I can't quite put my finger on it."

"Any word from Buster yet?" she asked in a whisper, but she knew full well it was too early for him to make it to the building closer to the bees, even at a dead run.

Darren shook his head.

"I was so sure we would find something in a truck," Reese whispered. "In the end, I'm just grasping at straws here, convincing myself we're going to find her."

Guilt reached all the way back to tenth grade, when she'd lost Camree Lynn.

"Something is off...what it is?" Darren asked. "Let's check the trucks one more time."

Considering they had no Plan B and it was too early to hear from Buster, they had nothing to lose by checking. This time, they worked in reverse. Truck number three revealed nothing different, but they got inside and walked through it, feeling around for something even though they had no idea what to look for.

Walking truck two, Reese got the same uneasy sense as Darren. "It's this one. Something is off."

She walked through it again.

"It's shorter than the other one," she said as Darren nodded. They walked to the back of the truck and felt around.

"I got something," Darren said as he bent down and reached for a handle. He cranked it as they heard a gasp.

Reese held her breath as he opened the panel. A teenager was curled in a space that was about two feet deep. There was a bottle of water and another bottle that looked like it was for urine. The smell was the first thing that struck Reese.

And then, two wide eyes blinked up at her as Darren turned the flashlight beam away from the girl's face.

"Tandra?" Reese asked, scanning the girl's body, looking for bindings. It stood to reason it would be her since years passed in between abductions and she was the most recent.

Tandra sat up, and scooted away from them. She had bindings on her wrists and feet. Wide-eyed, her face bleached-sheet white, she shook her head as though urging them to forget they'd ever seen her.

"It's okay," Reese soothed. "You're safe now. We're going to get you out of here and take you home."

Darren took a step back while Tandra's gaze stayed locked on to him. Fear radiated from the poor girl.

"He's not going to hurt you, Tandra," Reese said. "And neither am I."

Tandra's gaze finally shifted from Darren to Reese. The teen's chin quivered before the tears started to fall. She released a sob that cracked Reese's heart in half.

"I need you to be as quiet as you can, okay?" Reese

said, looking around for something to use to cut the bindings.

Darren produced a pocketknife but maintained a distance. In fact, he turned his back so he could face the opening of the truck, then palmed the gun he'd brought along with him. If anyone showed up in the opening, he would be ready for them.

Reese worked quickly, cutting the ropes off Tandra's wrists and ankles. The teen immediately lunged for Reese, wrapping her arms around Reese's neck in a death grip. "I've got you. You're going to be okay now. You're going home."

Tandra nodded but she didn't speak. The teen was crying softly and buried her face in Reese's shoulder. All they needed to do now was notify Buster, the law and then get the hell out of there.

DARREN HAD ENOUGH life experience—or maybe just plain old bad luck—not to take this find for granted. Locating her was only half the battle. The rest was getting off the property with Buster, with all four of them in one piece.

If anyone made too loud a noise, the dog would come unglued and wake up the house. The men on the east side of the property would be here in a heart-beat. They, no doubt, had some mode of transportation to get them from one section to the next while they hunted for trespassers.

Darren exited the truck first after shooting a text to Buster, and then waved Reese to follow suit. With the teen hanging on one side, Reese managed to get them both out of the vehicle without making much noise.

He scanned the area. It looked clear.

Moving to the tree line, the trio made their way toward the pickup. There'd been no return text or acknowledgment from Buster, and that had Darren worried. He wouldn't exactly call this extraction easy, but they seemed to be flying under the Archer family's radar for the time being.

With every step toward freedom, Tandra's sobs grew louder. Reese did her best to keep the teen quiet, but only so much could be done without her cooperation. At this point, the teen was most likely in shock. She was just a kid, doing her best after what had have been the most traumatic event in her life.

Darren's heart went out to her and her parents. Losing a child had to be a parent's worst nightmare, but having a kid abducted would be a close second.

But this wasn't the time to celebrate. He had a bad feeling deep in his gut. That Buster wasn't answering the text wasn't a good sign. The hairs on the back of his neck pricked again as the dark-cloud feeling returned, threatening to smother him.

He took the lead, keeping Reese and Tandra tucked right behind him as he moved through scrub brush toward the pickup.

Once they were safely out of earshot of the house, Reese asked, "Has Buster checked in?"

"I'm afraid not," Darren said. He could put these two inside the pickup, hand her his cell phone and go back for Buster.

Reese would protest the move, but they were short on options and even she would have to agree getting Tandra to safety had to be their first priority. She would also understand that he couldn't leave Buster on the property.

Breaking through the tree line onto the road, they cut right toward the pickup. Now that they were off property, Darren allowed himself a burst of hope that he could get this child through this ordeal. Could they call 911? If they did, was Buster as good as dead? Was he already?

Air squeezed out of Darren's lungs. Breathing hurt.

He gave himself a mental shake and kept moving.

Finally, the truck was in sight. All hope Buster might have dropped his cell phone or the battery died disappeared.

When the truck was twenty feet ahead, two large male figures stood up from squatting in front of the vehicle. Darren muttered a string of curses, palmed his cell and sent a 911 text. He could only hope it went through.

"If you're smart, you'll put your hands where I can see them," one of the men said. Darren recognized the voice as Alexander Archer's.

Tandra's cries became louder. That poor girl.

As much as Darren wished he could bum-rush these bastards, he couldn't. Two against one, especially when both of them were carrying guns, wasn't the kind of odds Darren could handle. If he was killed, where would that leave Reese and Tandra? He would be making his babies orphans.

"The law is already on its way," Darren said, hoping they wouldn't call his bluff. "Your only choice is to let us go. We'll say that we found her walking down the street and she won't say a word about where she's been or who had her. Just leave her alone and she won't talk."

"Nice try," the other one said. Darren recognized the voice as Aiden's. There was one more brother, but who knew where he was? He might not even live at home. "All three of you are coming with us."

"You won't get away with killing three people," Darren argued. "Think this through."

"We've gotten away with a whole lot more than that," Aiden said before being shushed by his older brother.

"Your mouth was always going to get us busted," Alexander admonished. "It's the reason Mama and Daddy keep you on the property while me and Andrew do all the work."

"Our brother isn't even here right now," Aiden complained. There was something simple yet threatening about the tone of his voice.

"He'll be back in a few days, and you need to be quiet," Alexander said, his tone more of a threat.

So, it was two against one at this point, since Reese had her hands full with Tandra. Speaking of Reese, he had an idea. He reached behind and placed the pistol, along with his cell, in the flat of Reese's palm. She got the idea and immediately gripped it. He pointed toward the tree line. They were close enough to zigzag through the trees to avoid being shot.

"You might as well stop hiding," Alexander said. "Come out, come out, wherever you are."

Darren stopped himself from pointing out they were standing in plain sight. With Andrew out of the picture, there was at least a little hope they could survive these twisted bastards. He took a small step back. The farther he could get them away from these jerks, the better chance all three of them had at getting out of this alive.

What he needed right now was a miracle. If he could get them close enough to the trees and distract them, Reese could run with Tandra.

"I told you to get your hands up," Alexander said, his voice filled with rage.

Darren complied. There wasn't anything to hide, anyway, now that Reese had the gun and cell phone. She also had the keys. Could Darren draw the men away from the ladies?

"Don't do it," Reese said so quietly that he almost didn't hear her. "Don't risk it. We'll figure something out."

"Now, send us the bitches and no one will get hurt," Alexander demanded. "It's just like Mama said. The only woman we can trust is her. The rest are evil just like Me-ma. Me-ma used to torture Mama. Now, all Mama was trying to do was find ones for us and teach them how to be good girls. She said we have to start young before they become too worldly."

One on one, Darren had no doubt he could take these men down despite their hefty size if they didn't have weapons. But as it was, one wrong move and one of the ladies behind him could end up paying the price.

"Hold on," Darren hedged, trying to stall for time.

"Time's up," Alexander said, weapon aimed at the center of Darren's chest while the man walked right toward him.

"Go," Darren said out of the corner of his mouth.

A second before Reese and Tandra could react, the buzz of a small airplane or helicopter came roaring up. The drone. It was the drone. That must mean Buster was alive. His condition was unknown, but he must still be breathing, conscious, and reasonably coherent.

The drone attacked Alexander, who waved his right arm around to stop it from smacking him in the face. Aiden's gaze was fixed on his brother, his mouth agape.

Darren didn't waste the chance to bolt into the tree line with Reese and Tandra. He stopped as soon as they reached cover, took the gun from Reese, aimed and fired. A look of shock stamped Aiden's features. It took a second for him to realize he'd been hit in the calf. He squatted down to one knee and used his hand to stop the blood squirting from his wound, dropping his weapon in the process.

If only Darren was closer, he would take the bastard's gun.

The drone was bouncing around, just out of reach for Alexander. Darren took aim and shot, hitting Alexander in the shoulder. He dropped his gun as he shrieked in pain.

"Freeze and I'll let you live," Darren shouted from the trees.

Aiden put up his hands in the surrender position. Alexander came gunning toward the trees. Darren had no choice but to shoot. This time, he hit his thigh, bringing him down.

A sound coming from behind said Darren's luck might have just run out.

# Chapter Twenty-Three

A deep growl came from behind Reese. She spun around and tucked Tandra behind her. Whatever came out of those trees would have to get through her first.

Darren handed her the gun one more time. "Shoot if you need to but know what or who you're shooting before you fire."

He was gone before she could tell him she had no idea how to handle a gun. *Point and shoot.* She'd played video games with her brothers when she was a kid. This must be close to the same thing. Right?

Not thirty seconds later, a figure emerged. Her finger hovered over the trigger mechanism. But then she froze.

"Buster," Reese said as he stumbled out from behind a tree. And then he collapsed. "Darren, it's him. He's alive."

With Tandra clinging to her, she ran toward him. A siren sounded in the distance, the welcome shrieks filling the air. This would also alert Mr. and Mrs. Archer, but Reese couldn't care about that right now. She needed to get Buster off the Archer property.

Reese dropped to her knees, not caring that she was stabbed by scrub brush in the process. Tandra stayed right beside Reese but let go of her neck, which was helpful. "Buster."

He didn't look as though he was breathing, so she unbuttoned the top couple of buttons on his shirt. His eyes were closed and his breathing shallow. She checked for a pulse and got one, but it was faint.

"What do I do?" Reese asked, searching her brain for something that could wake him up.

"Move over…" It was Tandra's tiny voice. "We learned CPR in school. Let me try something."

She pinched his nose, opened his mouth and blew measured breaths into it. Then, she switched gears, placed her fisted hands together on his chest and pumped as she counted.

And then she repeated time and time again, until paramedics arrived on the scene. The pair of young men, who looked to be in their early twenties, took over, and placed an oxygen mask over Buster's nose and mouth.

"You might have just saved a life," the EMT named Jerry said to Tandra. "I didn't catch your name."

"Tandra," she said.

Recognition dawned as Sheriff Courtright came jogging over.

"Tandra St. Claire?" the sheriff asked.

"Yes, sir," she responded as Buster was lifted onto a gurney. The teen was shaking by this point.

Jerry turned to Reese and said, "His vitals are good. It's looking good for him."

"Thank you," she said a moment before he was taken away. She scanned the area for Darren, and found him giving a statement to a deputy near where the Archer brothers had been cuffed and placed into the back of a service vehicle.

"The parents were inside the house," Reese said to the sheriff. "They're involved."

"I have a deputy heading that way now," Sheriff Courtright stated.

"There better be someone from animal control with him," she quipped.

The crack of a bullet split the air.

Tandra shrank.

"It's okay," Reese soothed. "You're going to be okay now."

"I want my momma," Tandra said, reverting back to what she probably called her mother as a child.

Reese looked to the sheriff.

"She needs to be checked over by a doctor," Reese pointed out, still in full-on protective mode.

"Yes, ma'am," the sheriff said. "We're heading to the ER where her parents will meet us after they've been informed."

Tandra seemed satisfied with the answer as she clung to Reese.

"What the hell was that?" Reese asked the sheriff as he listened to his radio. She clamped her eyes shut, afraid the dog had just been shot. Her chest squeezed.

The sheriff spoke quietly into the radio strapped to his shoulder. He turned to Reese and said, "A warning shot was fired by the Archers, but once they were informed their sons were going to jail, they surrendered."

"And their dog?" she asked.

"It's fine, but it'll need a new home once this family goes to jail," he said. "We plan to lock them up."

"Andrew Archer is out there somewhere but the others were clear about him being in on it," Reese informed the sheriff.

"We're tracking him down right now," the sheriff said. "So far, we believe he is unaware of the circumstances here."

"Someone needs to throw the book at him, too," she said, disgusted these murderers had gotten away with their crimes for so long.

"They said I was going to die," Tandra finally said. "Just like the others before me."

The teen released a sob as Reese did her best to soothe the young girl. Teenagers were caught in the space between being a child and an adult—it was a difficult time where they needed independence, but also needed to be watched more than ever.

"You're going to be just fine," Reese said, walking her over to the sheriff's SUV. She looked at the sheriff. "She's shivering." The teen had on jeans and a sweater that was filthy and had been ripped.

Reese also acknowledged what the teen had just said. *Just like the others before me* meant they were all gone. Tears overwhelmed Reese.

"I have a blanket in the back of my vehicle," he said, then went to retrieve it. As he walked away from them, he also communicated on the radio. Reese walked Tandra to the opened passenger door of his SUV.

"Sit inside here," Reese said, only able to focus on the teen right then. "This will keep you warm."

The heater was on, and this kiddo desperately needed to warm up.

"Don't leave," Tandra said as the sheriff returned.

"I won't," Reese promised. "I'm right here until your parents arrive."

Tandra nodded, then sniffled and wiped tearstained cheeks. "I never should have talked to him at the store."

"Who?" the sheriff asked.

Tandra gave her statement. By the time she finished, Reese was ready to throw a punch at one of those bastards presently in the back seat of the deputy's SUV wearing handcuffs. It was probably good that Courtright climbed inside the driver's seat and then pulled away. Justice would be served when the book was thrown at those jerks.

Darren walked over and stood behind Reese. She leaned back into his chest as he looped his arms around her. His body was all the warmth she needed. And yet, she also realized this was the end of it.

"You came asking questions on your way to the ranch," he said in her ear. "I overheard Alexander telling the deputy they had to stop you."

It explained why she'd been abducted and nearly murdered.

"But first, they intended to torture you by showing you where your best friend was buried. They planned to dig a grave next to her," he said quietly, reverently. "Nothing will ever happen to you on my watch."

Tears streamed down her cheeks. Tears for Camree Lynn. Tears for Tandra. Tears for the fact it was time to go home to the family ranch and face the music, leaving Darren behind. She would be leaving her heart behind with him.

That was life, though. It was messy and unpredictable, coming so close to giving her everything she could have ever wanted before ripping it all away again.

Walking away from Darren a second time was going to be the second hardest thing she'd ever done.

DARREN WATCHED AS Tandra's parents were reunited with their daughter in the ER. He listened as the fifteen-year-old detailed the Archers' plan to kill her by Christmas. The horror of what she'd gone through would last a lifetime, but she would sleep in her own bed tonight and that was something to be grateful for.

His cell buzzed, so he immediately answered. "Hello?"

"This is Jeanie," the familiar voice said. "I just thought you would want to know that Buster is going to be just fine."

"That's great news, Jeanie," he said to Buster's wife. "Really great news."

"If not for someone knowing how to administer CPR, then…"

Her voice cracked on the last word.

"I'll pass along the message," he said to her. "I'm sorry that I let him come with us."

"He wouldn't have taken no for an answer, but his heart isn't what it used to be," she explained.

"Then, we'll figure out a way to force him to rest," Darren said, realizing that by selling his personal home and moving into the ranch, he could afford to hire another hand to lighten the load. Ever since the twins, he'd been busy with his children and wasn't pulling his weight on the ranch. "Things are going to change for the better."

It was a promise he intended to keep.

"Thank you, Darren," she said. "I know how much you care about him, and he's such a mule. I've been asking him to talk to you for a while now."

"No need," he said. "I'm clear with what needs to happen. Plus, he can use a little more desk time. I hate managing the books. I'd much rather be outside more."

"I don't know what to say except thank you," she said.

"Loyalty means everything," he said to her. "Your husband was loyal to my parents and now to me. I won't let him down. You two are the only family I have left at the ranch."

They exchanged goodbyes before Darren ended the call. Change was in the air. And he had a few things to say to Reese before she walked out of his life forever.

The sheriff took a phone call. He said a few *uh-huhs* and an *I see* before thanking the caller and ending the call. "Looks like Andrew was pulled over on a minor traffic infraction and arrested. He went peacefully and said he would testify against his brothers. He's willing to cooperate for a lighter sentence."

"I don't know who he is," Tandra said honestly as her parents hugged her tight. She was waiting for the doctor to confirm she could go home.

Her father stepped up to Darren and Reese. He was a big man. Someone who looked proud. Tears ran down his face, and droplets stained his overalls.

"I don't know how to thank you for bringing me my little girl," he began with a shaky voice. "There's no way in the world I can ever repay something like this."

He didn't finish his sentence before Reese and Darren started shaking their heads.

"You don't owe us a thing," Darren said. "We are happy enough that your daughter is alive and well." Darren paused as emotion clotted in his throat. He looked Mr. St. Claire straight in the eyes and said, "I'm a father. Twin girls."

Mr. St. Claire nodded. He gave a look of understanding.

"I hope your girls stay safe," Mr. St Claire finally said. "And if they ever need an uncle or guardian angel…they can count on me."

Now, Darren was the one trying to hold back tears.

"It takes a village, right?" he asked but it was more statement than question.

"It sure does," Mr. St. Claire agreed before his daughter wrapped her arms around him. They weren't long enough to clasp her hands together, so she grabbed fist-fuls of his overalls.

"I won't ever talk to strangers online or otherwise and I'll never leave the house again without you and mom knowing where I'll be at all times," she promised.

"You did nothing wrong," her mother said. "But your father and I plan to be home every night, together, to take care of you."

Tandra beamed through big teary eyes.

The family of three huddled together.

"Are you ready to get out of here?" Darren asked, turning toward Reese.

"Yes," she said, then added, "But I'm not ready to leave you."

"Then don't," he said. "Let's go home and clean up. I'd like you to meet my girls before you go to back to your family's ranch."

"I'd like that very much," Reese said, warming his heart.

After saying their goodbyes, they walked outside and to his vehicle. She scooted over to the middle seat for the ride back to the farmhouse. They sat in companionable silence with her curled up against his arm.

Back home, they showered, ate and set up the place for his girls. He should probably be tired, but going to sleep meant losing his few precious hours with Reese before she walked out of his life again. They'd promised to be friends, but he knew as much as she that their schedules would make it a challenge to stay in touch.

Still, it was better than nothing.

By the time the house was set up, his former in-laws called. They were on the way, saying they wanted to check out the new space for the girls. Darren heard something in their voices that alarmed him, but he'd been running on adrenaline all night and tried not to read too much into it.

"Is it strange that I'm worried I'll make a bad impression on eighteen-month-olds?" Reese finally said after pacing around the room a couple of times.

"They don't always take to new people right away," he warned. "But don't let that put you off."

She nodded as a knock sounded. And then she followed him to the door before he opened it.

His former in-laws were normally put together to a T. His mother-in-law's hair was pinned in back and his father-in-law had bags underneath his eyes.

"Who are these angels?" Reese said as the girls were carried inside and then set down on the soft rug in the living room.

"Our granddaughters," his former mother-in-law Alice quipped.

Reese walked right over to her, extended a hand and introduced herself. Alice's eyes widened at the last name Hayes.

"It's a pleasure to meet you, Ms. Hayes," Alice said, taking the offering. "Darren didn't tell us it was you."

"Would it have made a difference?" he asked. It clearly did, considering Alice didn't answer. "Reese is going to be part of my life and I'd like her to know my girls."

Alice nodded but she was hiding something. He prepared himself for them to say they planned to fight him for custody.

"Let's clear the air, shall we?" he asked. "Before you fight me for custody you should know how much I love those girls and—"

"Oh, we do," Clifford Brown said. "And they are lucky to have you." Cliff shook his head. "We've had them for two nights and realized the amount of work they are."

"It's twenty-four-seven," Alice added. "Believe me when I say we are happy as larks being grandparents. We don't want to go back to being full-time parents. It's hard work."

Well, that news really made Darren laugh. But when he turned around to see Ivy reaching for Reese to hold her, his heart would never be the same.

"In fact, we don't want to be rude, but we'd like to go home and take a nap," Cliff said.

Then they all laughed, including the girls, who were clueless. He hoped to maintain their innocence for as long as humanly possible. But they were also going to be signed up for self-defense classes before their fifth birthday.

"Thank you for keeping them," he said, waving to Alice and Cliff as they couldn't get out of the house fast enough. He turned to Reese. "I guess that's settled."

Her smile lit a dozen campfires inside him.

"If you ever need a babysitter," she said as Iris cooed at her, "I'm your girl."

Darren wasn't sure if this was the right time, but he decided to throw caution and logic to the wind. Because those last three words spoken out of Reese's mouth made him want to make it a permanent arrangement.

"I know it's been a long time since we've known each other," he began, running with the first words that came to mind, "but I know you, Reese."

She practically beamed at him.

"And I know me, too," he said. "Being friends isn't going to be enough. Not when I haven't been able to find anyone else who holds a candle to you. I fell in love with you in high school and I've been in love with you ever since." His heart pounded the inside of his ribs with the next words. "I guess what I'm saying is that I don't ever want you to leave again."

Reese walked over to him.

"You would forgive me?" she asked, blinking those beautiful eyes up at him.

"Already done," he said. And it was the truth. "I can't push away the woman I love."

"Because I don't think I ever stopped loving you, either," she admitted. "And now, these girls, it just feels like the family I'm supposed to have."

Darren dropped down on one knee. "Then, I have one question for you."

Tears welled in her eyes before rolling down her cheeks.

"Will you marry me?" he asked.

"Yes," she said, pulling him up to standing. "I love you and I would be proud to be your wife."

Coming home was exactly what Darren and his girls needed. With Reese, his family was complete.

# *Epilogue*

Darren wasn't sure he wanted to wait any longer for the lab results. In fact, getting the pediatrician involved might have been a mistake. "I'm not sure any of this is necessary. These are my girls and no test can say—"

"I know," Reese reassured him. "*We* know. But there could be medical history questions that come up later, and they need to know. It's just biology, Darren. *You* are their father, and they love you."

He nodded, tapping his fingers on the chair of the waiting room of the pediatrician's office.

The door leading to the exam rooms opened and a nurse appeared.

"Darren," she said, smiling warmly at him. Was that a good sign?

He stood up, linked fingers with Reese and followed her into the green exam room.

"The doctor will be with you shortly," the nurse said. He should know her name by now. It felt like he'd been in here every other week during these first eighteen and a half months.

"Can you check the chart?" he asked her.

"I'm afraid not," she said before closing the door behind her.

The door barely closed when it opened again.

"Hey, Dr. Michaels," Darren said. "This is my fiancée, Reese."

"Pleased to meet you," Dr. Michaels said to her. The two exchanged pleasantries. He had an envelope tucked underneath his arm. He grabbed it and held it up after closing the door and washing his hands.

Darren took in a deep breath. No matter what that envelope said, he was the one who'd changed their diapers. He was the one who'd sat up with them when they couldn't sleep. And he was the one who'd promised their mother that he would never walk away from those girls.

Dr. Michaels opened the envelope and scanned the contents. He handed over the top piece of paper. "I'm sorry to say the probability that you're the biological father of Iris and Ivy is almost none."

"Which doesn't change a thing," Darren quickly said. "I'm still their father in every way that matters."

"No, it doesn't," Reese added. "And, yes, you are."

"Hazel mentioned to me during one of her solo visits that it might come to this test someday," Dr. Michaels said. "She asked me to keep the information confidential, so I honored her request."

"She talked to you about him?" Darren asked.

"I have an address," he said. "If you're interested." Darren nodded.

The doctor handed over a slip of paper. "You'll let

me know if this changes anything about their care, right?"

"Absolutely," Darren said. "I will always want what is best for them."

"It's your name on the birth certificate," Dr. Michaels pointed out.

"They deserve to know the truth," Darren stated. He folded up the piece of paper and thanked the doctor, then they left.

"Where are we headed?" Reese asked.

"Nowhere," he said. "There's a phone number."

He stopped at the SUV and stood on the sidewalk before opening the slip. He fished out his cell phone and made the call.

"Speak," a hard, gruff voice said. He coughed like he'd just smoked a pack of cigarettes.

"Do you know Hazel Montgomery?" Darren asked.

"I knew her," he said and then seemed to catch on. "But those kids aren't mine. And even if they were, I'd want nothing to do with them."

"Are you sure about that?" Darren asked.

The man belched.

"I'm a rocker and a drunk," he finally said before the sound of a bottle crashing against the wall interrupted him. "Oh, hell. That's going to cost me. But, no, I told Hazel when she first said she was pregnant to go the hell away."

"Hazel died a year ago," Darren informed him.

The guy released a string of swear words.

"But not before having twin girls," he continued.

"I'm the man she was married to when she had an affair with you."

Those words should be bitter, but he realized he'd never fully given Hazel his heart even though he'd wanted to.

"Like I said, I want nothing to do with them," the jerk said.

"Then I'll send over paperwork to make it official," Darren stated.

"Fine by me," the guy said. "That everything?"

"As a matter of fact, yes, it is." Darren ended the call before looking toward his future. "He doesn't care about them."

"His loss," she said, "because they are two little miracles."

"Our miracle babies," he said, then kissed his fiancée. "I like the sound of that."

Reese pulled back. "Are you ready to go home to our family, and then to mine to see why I've been called back to Cider Creek?"

"I thought you'd never ask."

\* \* \* \* \*

*Look for* Murder in Texas, *the final book in*
USA TODAY *bestselling author Barb Han's*
*miniseries The Cowboys of Cider Creek,*
*on sale next month!*

*And if you missed the previous titles in*
*the series, you can find them now wherever*
*Harlequin Intrigue books are sold!*

Rescued by the Rancher
Riding Shotgun
Trapped in Texas
Texas Scandal

# HARLEQUIN
## PLUS

Try the best multimedia
subscription service for romance
readers like you!

---

## Read, Watch and Play.

Experience the easiest way to get
the romance content you crave.

Start your **FREE TRIAL** at
<u>www.harlequinplus.com/freetrial</u>.